Tom, Tom, the piper's son,
Stole a pig and away did run;
The pig was eat
And Tom was beat,
And Tom went howling down
the street.

This colourful book presents fourteen of the best-loved nursery rhymes.

Each rhyme is printed in large, clear type and bold, bright pictures illustrate the familiar characters.

Young children will love to learn and repeat their favourite nursery rhymes again and again using this book.

Available in Series S808

* **a is for apple**
* **I can count**
Tell me the time
Colours and shapes
* **Nursery Rhymes**

**Also available as* Ladybird Teaching Friezes

Published by Ladybird Books Ltd Loughborough Leicestershire UK
Ladybird Books Inc Auburn Maine 04210 USA
© LADYBIRD BOOKS LTD MCMLXXXI
Printed in England

nursery rhymes

illustrated by LYNN N GRUNDY

Ladybird Books

Three blind mice,
  see how they run!
They all ran after
  the farmer's wife;
She cut off their tails
  with a carving knife,
Did ever you see such
  a thing in your life,
As three blind mice?

Little Bo-Peep
    has lost her sheep,
And doesn't know
    where to find them;
Leave them alone
    and they'll come home,
Wagging their tails
    behind them.

Old Mother Hubbard
Went to the cupboard,
To get her poor dog a bone;
But when she got there
The cupboard was bare
And so the poor dog had none.

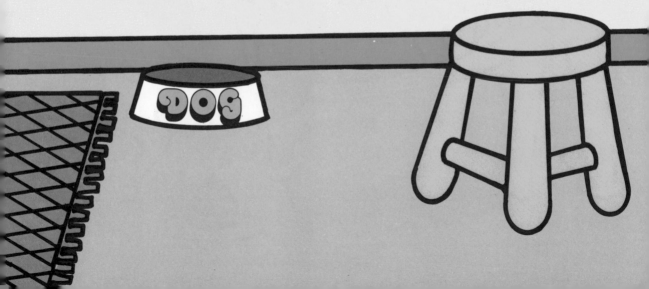

Rub-a-dub-dub,
Three men in a tub,
And who do you think
they be?
The butcher, the baker,
the candlestick-maker;
Turn them out,
knaves all three.

Old King Cole
Was a merry old soul,
And a merry old soul was he;
He called for his pipe,
And he called for his bowl,
And he called for his
    fiddlers three.

Mary, Mary, quite contrary,
How does your garden grow?
With silver bells
   and cockle shells
And pretty maids all in a row.

Little Miss Muffet
Sat on a tuffet,
Eating her curds and whey;
There came a big spider,
Who sat down beside her
And frightened
        Miss Muffet away.

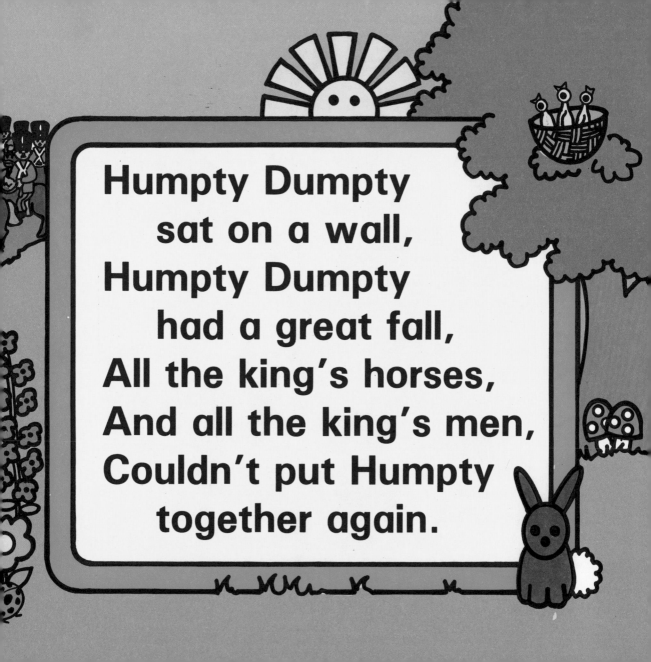

Humpty Dumpty
  sat on a wall,
Humpty Dumpty
  had a great fall,
All the king's horses,
And all the king's men,
Couldn't put Humpty
  together again.

Hey diddle diddle,
The cat and the fiddle,
The cow jumped
    over the moon;
The little dog laughed
To see such fun,
And the dish ran away
    with the spoon.

Little Jack Horner
Sat in a corner,
Eating his Christmas pie;
He put in his thumb,
And pulled out a plum,
And said,
   "What a good boy am I!"

There was an old woman
who lived in a shoe,
She had so many children
she didn't know what to do;
She gave them some broth
without any bread;
Then whipped them all soundly
and sent them to bed.

Baa, baa, black sheep,
Have you any wool?
Yes, sir, yes, sir,
Three bags full;
One for the master,
And one for the dame,
And one for the little boy
Who lives down the lane.

Care of the Dying

PRIORY EDITORIAL CONSULTANTS

THE CARE AND WELFARE LIBRARY

Consultant Medical Editor: Alexander R. K. Mitchell
MB, ch.B, MRCPE, MRCPsych.

Care of the Dying

Richard Lamerton

MRCS, LRCP

St. Joseph's Hospice, Hackney

(Illustrated by Harold Bisby)

Foreword by

Dr. Cicely Saunders, OBE, MRCP
St. Christopher's Hospice, Sydenham

PRIORY PRESS LIMITED

The Care and Welfare Library

The Alcoholic and the Help he Needs Max M. Glatt, MD, FRCPsych., MRCP, DPM

Drugs: The Parents' Dilemma Alexander R. K. Mitchell, MB, ch.B, MRCPE, MRCPsych.

Schizophrenia Alexander R. K. Mitchell, MB, ch.B, MRCPE, MRCPsych.

Sex and the Love Relationship Faith Spicer, MB, BS, JP

VD Explained Roy Statham, MB, ch.B

The Care of the Aged Dennis Hyams, MB, FRCP

The Child Under Stress Edna Oakeshott, Ph.D

Student Health Philip Cauthery, MB, ch.B, DPH

I.Q.—150 Sydney Bridges, MA, MEd., Ph.D

Stress in Industry Joseph L. Kearns, MB, BCh., MSC

Health in Middle Age Michael Green, MA, MB, BCh.

Children in Hospital Ann Hales-Tooke, MA

Healing Through Faith Christopher Woodard, MRCS, LRCP

The Baby's First Days James Partridge, MA, MB, BCh.

Sexual Variations John Randall, MD, FRCP

Depression: the Blue Plague C. A. H. Watts, OBE, MD

SBN 85078 080 2 (Hardback)
Copyright © 1973 by Richard Lamerton
First published in 1973 by
Priory Press Limited
101 Grays Inn Road London WC1
Made and printed in Great Britain by
The Garden City Press Limited
Letchworth, Hertfordshire SG6 1JS

Contents

Illustrations

Foreword

There are many who would like to help dying people and their families and who do not know how to begin. This includes relatives and friends as well as nurses and others professionally concerned. Many of us have heard the cry "I feel so helpless," or the sad admission "I ran away—I was afraid."

Dr. Lamerton has set out to give guidelines and practical advice to all those who are concerned to help people who are dying. To do this he has summarized work of many different kinds and from a wide variety of sources. He presents the results of research, of intuition and of practice and gives us an exhaustive list of references to start us on our further reading. But above all he speaks from the bedside and he is at his most stimulating when he produces some of the countless comments made to him by his patients. Nothing can teach us the care of the dying so clearly as can the dying themselves. Dr. Lamerton helps those he has known to reach a far wider audience as they express their longing and their loneliness but, above all, their courage, their common-sense and their acceptance.

Dying is part of living but too many make a lonely journey towards it because others leave them in isolation. Many will find that Dr. Lamerton's pungent style makes them think in new ways and gives them more confidence in drawing near to the mortally ill. Not all will agree with everything he says. How could they when he writes in such a personal way? Such a style may make him vulnerable, but it is this kind of writing which presses others into looking again at their own honesty and concern for patients. Because he is an enthusiast who gives us a number of dogmatic statements, Dr. Lamerton stimulates us to test and try for ourselves.

It is always an uncanny moment when the body, which even in confusion and distress has expressed the person, is suddenly empty. To me, the mind and body are inextricably interwoven, but

7

they appear to be no more than the tools of the spirit which finally lays them down when death comes. Dr. Lamerton directs us to look at this moment and in doing so to have new thoughts concerning the dignity of man.

The chapter on the role of religion, with its distillation of truths from different faiths, presents us with a special challenge. We are "to speak the truth as we know it at the time, fresh and alive, precisely appropriate to the man and his present needs."

But how can we, when we feel so helpless?

Sometimes we have to bear our inability to understand, to feel as if we are not helping at all and yet still go on staying close to a patient. It may be our very feeling of helplessness which enables us to meet him on the same level, and often we will find ourselves acknowledging that help has come to the two of us together.

Whatever the religious background of our patients we see them over and over again reaching out trustfully to what they see as true. They recall things from the past including much that they have been too busy to listen to before, and as death approaches they sometimes find that things begin to make sense. We see them bring a new attention to the old truths that belong to them. It is all an extremely personal matter for each patient and something entirely different from grasping at straws in panic.

We see also in dying persons (and this not only because we hope to see it) the fruit of the Spirit—"love, joy, peace, long-suffering, gentleness, goodness, faith, meekness, self-control" (*Galatians* 5:22). For us, this is truth, something we may see if we are there to do so. This reaffirms not only our faith in people but also our faith in the Christian God who died and rose again—the Truth of this moment of truth.

"Yes, doctor, you can show my photograph to anyone you like," I remember Mrs. C. saying, "and you can say to them 'it was all right'." When she came to St. Joseph's Hospice it was not "all right" for her but as she found her way it became "all right." It was she who was giving the answers, not the other way round. Answers are found by meeting life, not by demanding "Why?" but by asking "How?"—"How do I live in this situation?" It is like Victor Frankl finding meaning in the life of the concentration camps; like Dag Hammarskjold deciding to say "Yes" to life; it is learning with Pierre Teilhard de Chardin to accept our passivities at the deepest level. But for Mrs. C. it was not complicated like that at all. The answer for her was just simple, loving obedience to the daily demands of what was going on in a place where she was continually finding help and meaning, finding that "love casts out fear."

This book will help some of us to be more simple, and to respond better to the daily needs of dying patients. It will certainly make many look—perhaps for the first time—not only at the positive ways in which we can help them, but also at the treasures which they give us.

CICELY SAUNDERS

St. Christopher's Hospice, April 1973

Our Lady's Hospice, Harold's Cross, Dublin

Introduction

THE following letter appeared in the *Sunderland Echo*, a newspaper of County Durham, in August, 1972 :[212]

"Your correspondent Richard Lamerton states that he works in a hospice where the dying are cared for free from pain, without any clouding of consciousness. By modern techniques, he writes, this is perfectly possible, and dying can be a joyful process.

"It would be interesting to learn more of these techniques, which Dr. Lamerton suggests we use our pens to press for rather than for euthanasia. Why, one wonders, would a hospice have what apparently our hospitals do not have?

"Recently an old friend of mine died in hospital, after several months in great pain. She was given the maximum amount of pain killers, but nevertheless the slightest movement of her body was agonizing. Each time I visited her during her last weeks she said 'I wish I could die.' She was eighty-one. . . . I write to express the hope that Dr. Lamerton really knows his subject and is prepared to enlighten the public regarding this joyful process of dying."

This book is the result of my taking up the challenge.

Care of the Dying as a separate branch of medicine is in its infancy. One hopes it will not develop into a medical specialty, for although new techniques and teaching are often based on special units, their aim has been to see these directed back into general medical and nursing training.

My acknowledgements include my thanks to the *Nursing Times* for permission to quote sections of articles of mine published in December, 1972. Also I would like to thank the patients and staff of St. Joseph's Hospice in Hackney and St. Christopher's Hospice in Sydenham for giving me so much help in preparing this book, and for showing me how dying can indeed be a joyful experience. In particular my thanks are due to Miss M. Delaney and Mrs. W. Burns for help with manuscript preparation.

To add to the value of this handbook I have given a large number of references to other material on the subject—and rather than give footnotes on the pages themselves I have keyed the passages concerned to the numbered list of references at the back of the book.

Ardenlea Marie Curie Home, Ilkley, Yorkshire

I

The Needs

IT IS never true that "nothing more can be done" for a patient. It may be useless to continue treatment with curative drugs or surgery, but one can still give attention and friendship, relief and comfort.[128, 135] Sometimes a dying patient in hospital is looked on by the staff as one of their failures, while if he is at home, the nursing may prove too heavy for his family.

When a man is dying, active treatment of disease becomes increasingly irrelevant to his real needs. In the case of progressive incurable illness, the last three months of life are generally regarded as the period called "dying." It is, however, difficult to assess with any accuracy the duration of life left to a man.[163]

With good care, a patient can die without distress. Techniques are available whereby pain can be relieved, as can most of the other unpleasant symptoms which we commonly associate with dying. Nausea, for instance, and breathlessness can at least be eased until they are no longer in the forefront of the patient's attention. If there is physical distress as death approaches, it is probably because these newly-developed techniques which could bring relief are not being used.

The Need for Teaching

Terminal care involves a complete change of priorities for doctors and nurses. Their aim is now no longer to cure the patient, instead they work to keep him comfortable and both the medical and emotional needs of the patient have to be met effectively.

Nurses and medical students all over the world need teaching in this field.[41, 55, 114] The student who stands tongue-tied before a dying man realizes how little he understands the patient's needs or how to cope with them. He will probably learn most from an interdisciplinary discussion group, for in their care of the dying the doctor, priest and nurse have much to learn from each other.[95]

The Need for Hospices

Many people die peacefully in their sleep, requiring little or no medical attention. Half of the British population die in hospital. Those who die quickly from such causes as accidents, strokes, suicide or heart attacks do not involve the hospital staff in any change of priorities, and can be cared for in the everyday working. The elderly who die gently in the embrace of the "Old Man's Friend" (pneumonia—see p. 77), can usually be cared for at home by the family doctor and his team—again with no difficulty. But there will always be those who, like King Charles,[127] are "an unconscionable time a-dying," and whose demise is likely to be attended by distress.

For instance, one in five of us will die of cancer, occupying 9% of the non-psychiatric hospital beds.[180] Special care will be needed if the cancer proves painful (which often it does not). Other people who may need specialized terminal care are some of those with certain neurological diseases—such as multiple sclerosis or motor neurone disease—which may, if they progress severely enough, lead to the death of the patient. Other smaller groups needing this care would include a few of the people suffering from kidney, heart or liver failure, or brain injuries from accidents. Most of my observations have been made with the larger group, the cancer patients, though of course a diagnosis of cancer does not necessarily mean a death warrant: all manner of cures are now possible.

This period of terminal illness is very wearying for the patients, both physically and mentally, and is often a time when they receive much less medical and social support than they require.[182] Cottage hospitals, staffed by local family doctors, may sometimes be an enormous help,[176] particularly in country districts. To fill this gap in health care in towns, however, institutions called Hospices have come into being. The patient who does not need the manifold and costly resources of a general hospital and who cannot be at home is frequently better cared for, and happier, in a smaller specialized unit.[148, 189, 209, 242] Estimates of the number of beds required vary from two dozen to ten dozen per million of the population.[6, 243] Such a unit was originally called a "Hospice" by Mother Mary Aikenhead, a saintly Irish nun of the last century who founded the order of the Irish Sisters of Charity. She saw a parallel between a terminal home and the mediaeval houses of hospitality for pilgrims on their journey to the Holy Land which were also called "Hospices." These nuns and other Christian groups ran a few such homes for sixty years and then, just recently, the idea became more widespread. Now hospices are being opened in many centres all round the world. Usually they combine care of the dying with some other aspect of chronic or geriatric care or rehabilitation. This helps to avoid a rather macabre reputation as a coffin shop in the local neighbourhood, and keeps up the morale of both patients and staff. Many of these units do not call themselves hospices, preferring the word "home," but "hospice" is a useful generic name.

The service given by a hospice is two fold. In the wards patients are given the specialized medical and nursing care which had become impossible at home : and through its out-patients clinic it supports patients being cared for at home who might otherwise have had to die in hospital.

As you can see in Figure A (p. 48), which was prepared from studies of fifteen hundred patients who came to a hospice, 99% of those most recently admitted who had severe pain on admission were afforded relief, the rest having only occasional pain on unexpected movement. This was a group of patients selected from a wide area of London, whose suffering had previously not been controlled. One third of them were transferred from other hospitals. It can be seen that the figures improved as experience was gained and yet further improvement can be expected.

Other statistics, collected in general hospitals, showed that about one-fith of dying patients were in severe pain. Figures given in several surveys[63, 93, 196] reveal much suffering which we should be able to relieve. If the patient is cared for at home the prospect may be worse. In 1952 it was found that 68% of patients with cancer who were being looked after at home had severe or moderate suffering,[4, 130] and in 1972 Dewi Rees, a family doctor, found that 44% of his dying patients had continuous pain in spite of his own concern for the problem.[178]

By out-patient liaison with a hospice, this figure can be reduced to below 10%. Of those needing admission to the ward, less than 1% will still have pain which can be relieved only by reducing the patient's awareness. It is unlikely that corresponding figures from other countries would show much, if any, improvement on these British ones.

On the whole a general hospital is not the best place for a patient in need of special terminal care. So often he finds himself either hidden in a lonely side room or else exposed to a ward of thirty or more patients who are having surgical operations or making tantalizing recoveries while he goes downhill.

It is difficult, in a busy ward, with all its demands on the staff, to give a dying patient the understanding of his problems and the discriminating handling of the drugs that he needs to ease his symptoms. Inevitably much distress which could be relieved has to be overlooked. What is needed is a team of doctors and nurses with time just to sit and listen[64] : time to sort out symptoms and any other personal problems, time to help the patient to understand and adjust to his situation at his own pace. This applies equally to other members of the staff. There must be sensitive communication among the whole caring team—doctor, nurse, social worker, chaplain, physiotherapist and so on—so that as the patient's insight into his condition increases, his progress may be fully known to everyone who approaches him. Such a close-knit team is less likely to arise in a general hospital than in a small establishment like a hospice. A "terminal ward" tacked on to a big hospital would also have its disadvantages : other staff in the hospital would not always have the enlightened attitude to the dying which would be developed in those working in the unit, and if there were staff shortages, acute wards would naturally take precedence. For the patient the move would have the same significance as would a move to a hospice.

The Need for Research

Although it is now possible to relieve much of the suffering of the dying, many unanswered questions still remain. More research is urgently needed. It took some years to break the back of pain, and there is still room for improvement. Other symptoms need further carefully controlled trials, and the field of psychotherapy—both for the dying and for the bereaved—is being explored. We do not yet know enough about the process of normal healthy death, let alone about its pathology.

The needs of dying people were summarized in his survey of British terminal care in 1960 by Hughes[97] as being companionship, a sense of security, and control of physical symptoms by medical, nursing and domestic care. If these needs cannot be met at home, then the best place for the patient is a hospice.

At community level, there is a need for more teaching of and research into the care of the dying, so that one day we may all say with Francis Bacon,

"It is as natural to die as to be born."[14]

St. Columba's Hospital, Hampstead Heath, London

2

Teamwork

MODERN doctors and nurses cannot work in isolation. They need a host of other ancillary workers. Gradually the doctor's role is emerging as that of a team leader, the co-ordinator of what Sir Theodore Fox called "The Greater Medical Profession,"[67] a term embracing doctors in all specialties, with nurses, physiotherapists, occupational therapists, social workers, laboratory technicians, radiographers, speech therapists and so on.

Who are the Team?

If robots could replace men, A would look after B, and their roles would be distinct. But in real life nothing is so clear-cut. We have the situation in which a dying man's needs must be met, and everyone who contributes to or benefits from this situation is one of the team. Everyone involved has the opportunity to care and to learn. Each can be of help to the other. The team seen in this way— as including everyone who is contributing to the situation—becomes a much more alive, intelligent and human concept. It will include not only the hospital staff and family doctor team, but also the relatives and friends of the patient and, note this, the patient himself. How this can work, I will illustrate with the story of a Mrs. N.

This lady in her forties had come from the West Indies with four of her older children so that they could be well educated and gain professional qualifications. After a few years she was found to have a breast cancer. The breast was removed, and so were the ovaries in an effort to arrest the malignant process. Unfortunately, however, in her case this failed, and so did radiotherapy. The cancer spread to her liver and bones, making her feel very ill, and giving rise to great pain. When she came into our care, she commented, "I had an operation for my breast and now my liver is big," clearly indicating that she appreciated her diagnosis. She said she would love to see her children in Grenada, but didn't suppose she ever would now, though her passport and vaccinations were up to date.

Having relieved her pain, we made tentative enquiries as to how the money for a flight home to Grenada might be found. One by one we met the family and heard of her hopes for each. She said the oldest boy had turned out to be a "bad lot" and had little to do with his mother, leaving her very concerned that the other two boys should not fall into similar ways. In particular the younger, P., was beginning to keep bad company. So when we pointed out that she was too weak to fly alone, she chose young P. to be her companion on the plane, reasoning that if she could get him away from London he could work on his father's farm in moral safety. Most of the money was raised by her son named B., and her daughter—who were both now working. The last £100 was kindly contributed by the National Society for Cancer Relief.

The complications were phenomenal. There was the night Mrs. N. panicked and thought she would die before seeing home again; the cajoling of the customs to let through her two litre-bottles of heroin mixture!; the forklift to get her wheelchair on board the plane, and finally the losing of young P. in the air terminal, which delayed the flight.

We received a triumphant letter from Grenada some weeks later. She had pain again but obviously considered it unimportant. A fortnight later she died, just three days after seeing her second daughter married in Grenada. Then the following September her son B. turned up at the Hospice asking for work as a ward orderly, because he said it seemed a good place to be. When he moved on six months later, he told me that it was the first job from which he had never taken a day off.

Now who, in this story, was caring for whom? The decisions were all Mrs. N's, every stage being discussed frankly with her. This is what I mean by a team approach. Life presented a problem, and all the people involved contributed what they could to deal with it responsibly.

"In giving himself time to meet his patient thus, the doctor will so often find that he himself gains more than he gives. It is from the dying that we learn to care for the dying."[193] All that distinguishes the patient from the rest of the team is that his role in the play is that of dying.

In Britain today the patient is frequently told nothing about his diagnosis—he may even be told lies—yet his closest relatives are nearly always told. This is a hopelessly mechanical way of doing things, since the first person to be told should obviously be the one most able to take it. The patient may be the strongest member of the family, and may need to help them to accept the situation. Far from being supported by strong family relationships, however, the dying man often finds himself cut off by a wall of deception. The family are one moment preparing and planning for a world without him in it, and the next are talking about "when you get better." This can be very hard on a husband or wife who for decades has shared all troubles with the patient.[15] If this situation has been allowed to arise, it may be necessary to break down these barriers, very gently, to enable the couple to say their farewells. It is important to say goodbye. A conspiracy of silence will worsen the dying person's sense of isolation and stores up later emotional problems for the bereaved.[236] On the other hand of course, many patients will make it clear that they don't want to think about disease at all, and will leave everything to the doctor. This is just as valid, but at least the patient should be given the opportunity to choose which approach he would like to take.

Some relatives will be very obviously part of the caring side of the team, some will equally obviously be patients along with the dying man, and yet others will alternate between the two roles. It may be that they will need to be put up in the hospital overnight— as when they are too distressed to return home alone, or when they want to be close at hand if death is imminent.

While it would not be appropriate for them to read the patient's notes, which are worded for trained eyes only, relatives should be kept clearly in the picture—usually by a ward sister. If given the chance, they will have so many questions: Did he ask if he had

cancer yesterday? What was he told? Why was his blood transfusion stopped? Do our visits tire him? How long has he to live
now? To the extent that they are also patients, relatives need to
be cared for as well. For this reason one or two hospices have a
"relatives' day off" when visiting of all but the most severely ill
patients is discouraged. This releases the visitor who feels it is his
duty to be with his loved one as much as possible, so that he never
gets out. Visiting is otherwise unrestricted, of course, and this gives
rise to no problems for the nursing staff.[101]

In the next two chapters I shall consider the contributions of all
the other members of the team who constitute the "Greater Medical
Profession," and if one is fortunate enough to be supported by the
goodwill of an army of voluntary workers, they also have a most
valuable part to play. It may be economical to have a full-time
organizer to recruit and deploy this help. I remember Mrs. B., an
old lady with extensive bone cancer whose hair had fallen out as a
side-effect of some of the treatment she had been given. She spent
Christmas Day covered in blushes and giggles because a hairdresser
produced a wig for her, splendidly permed. It is worthwhile to
keep a stock of wigs, spectacles, magnifying glasses, hearing aids
and such like—discarded by ex-patients—for the purpose of helping
present ones to live their last few weeks of life more fully. It would
take too long, and be rather wasteful, to get new ones from the
social services.

When unpleasant symptoms are under control and the patient
is able to return home from hospital for a while, then a social
worker can be the liaison between the two and can help to deal with
the economic consequences of a disease which has wiped out a
person's earning capacity.[22] All civil and financial worries should
be resolved before he dies.

But there are bigger problems than this. One question always
asked when someone is admitted to a hospital is, "What's your
religion?" Many of the "nominal C of E" group lapsed after the
war, while several have said to me "I believe in Jesus, but I
wouldn't go to church." Nearly all of them appreciate a visit from
a clergyman. Provided he is a familiar figure in the wards, his
approach will not be accorded any dark significance. Ideally there
should be a full-time hospital chaplain, whose role is that of another
listener, who is particularly in tune with crises of conscience. The
actual sectarian bent of the minister/priest/rabbi involved in such

21

work is largely irrelevant provided he is obviously a clergyman and can listen.[13] Once a particular cleric is found to be helpful, he is a very important member of the team caring for the dying. He should be consulted whenever possible, and such medical information as he needs confided in him,[246] for the patient may choose to speak frankly to any member of the team—ward sister, doctor, chaplain, social worker or physiotherapist.[52] And if he were to ask about his diagnosis or prognosis, uninformed embarrassed confusion may silence for ever the question which carries the most potential for relief of the patient's uncertainty, frustration and fears.

In other words, the doctor's ivory tower is crumbling. And so it should if the physical and spiritual comfort of the patient is in question. Medicine, after all, is no longer in charge of the situation : death is taking over. No amount of professional tradition, etiquette or administrational difficulty, however heavy, can be an excuse for failing to minister to the self-evident needs of a dying man.

A man who wishes to prepare himself for death may need help. Which member of the team he chooses to confide in is entirely his own affair. More-senior staff need not be offended because he did not speak to them. Indeed, if none of the hospital staff wins his trust, they should be ready to call in the family doctor or district nurse, who may have known the patient for many years. At the end of one of his excellent papers Professor John Hinton stressed this need for good communication between all the people concerned with the care of a person who is dying.[93]

The Roles Overlap

Clearly the roles of doctor, priest and nurse are not going to be in neat compartments, for at times they will be completely interchangeable.[135] To be instantly responsive to the patient's needs one requires nurses who can alter the dosage of drugs, recognize when to give a wide range of "when necessary" prescriptions, and insert a urinary catheter. One needs doctors who can also be spiritual advisers and clergymen who can competently impart a grave prognosis. It is the widening of the scope of one's work, closer to the traditional role of the old-time family doctor, which is the principal attraction in care of the dying.

It is a sphere in which one will inevitably find nurses teaching doctors, and vice versa. The needs of the situation are so obvious that petty divisions become unimportant. An example of good communication in one hospice is the "pink sheet" to be found in each patient's notes. On this are recorded any significant comments made by a patient which may reveal the progress of his growing insight into his condition. Any member of the staff may write on this sheet or use it for reference.

Nurses in general hospitals may be uneasy about some of the doctor's decisions in the care of dying patients : Why were Mrs. Whatsit's antibiotics stopped? Why can't Mr. Overthere be left in peace instead of having all those tubes pushed in every orifice? Nurses need help with what to say to the dying patient[141] and what is to be their own attitude to death. The best person to deal with these problems is often a chaplain who is versed in medical ethics. Diffident nurses who will not question the medical staff can go to him, and he can help the two groups to communicate with each other over the nurses' ethical dilemmas.

A Partnership of Equals

The following is part of an essay[92] dictated by Enid Henke, a lady dying of motor neurone disease who was herself too weak to write :

"A friend and I were considering life and its purpose. I said, even with increasing paralysis and loss of speech I believed there was a purpose for my life but I was not sure what it was at that particular time.... After a while my friend said, 'It must be hard to be the wounded Jew when by nature you would rather be the Good Samaritan.'

It is hard : It would be unbearable were it not for my belief that the wounded man and the Samaritan are inseparable. It was the helplessness of the one that brought out the best in the other and linked them together.

In reflecting on the parable I am particularly interested in the fact that we are not told the wounded man recovered. I have always assumed that he did but it now occurs to me that even if he did not recover the story would still stand as a perfect example of true neighbourliness. You will remember that the story concludes with the Samaritan* asking the innkeeper to take care of the man, but he assures him of his own continuing interest and support : so the innkeeper becomes linked. . . ."

Enid was another patient who, one felt, was caring for the staff

* Luke 10:29–37.

while they cared for her. In exploring the answer to my question, "Who is caring for whom?" I remembered how often patients may care for one another, with reassurance, example and friendship. Then I remembered how patients like Enid can care for the staff by being considerate of their feelings, and by just accepting service.[208] And finally there came to mind all the ways the staff can help one another by discussion and the sharing of experience and troubles.

This, then, is the team which stands ready to serve and to encourage the dying patient. Though they work in much the same way as with recuperating patients, the emphasis is different. Always before them, the focal point and perfectly appropriate conclusion to their whole work, is a special moment—perhaps months away, perhaps tomorrow—when the patient will die. To this moment all their efforts will be directed, that it may be peaceful, joyful and contented.

Edenhall Marie Curie Home, London N.W.3

3

Dying at Home

Dying persons gain so much by being cared for by an affectionate family; they are better able to maintain themselves as individuals. Remaining at home, not swallowed up in the possible anonymity of the dying hospital patient, they need not doubt they are still part of the family. While among their family, they do not consider themselves as hulks awaiting the end, as long as they can participate, even in a limited role.—Professor John Hinton's Pelican Book, *Dying*, p. 153.

EVERY year over forty thousand people in Britain die at home, the majority suffering no great hardship.[241, 243] For the minority, however, pressing needs do emerge. These were well documented by the Marie Curie Memorial Foundation and the Queen's Institute of District Nursing who carried out a joint survey in 1952 in order to know where to deploy the resources of the new Marie Curie Fund. Some 7,050 patients were involved in this painstaking and detailed research work, and most of its findings are still relevant today.[130] The need for hospices and convalescent homes, for cancer education, for the co-ordinating of social work agencies, and for home

25

helps were clearly seen. There was also an urgent need for night nurses.

The Foundation lost no time in implementing the findings. Their first hospice was opened in the same year—the Tidcombe Hall Home in Tiverton, Devon. The Area Welfare Grant Scheme made money available to district nurses for the urgent needs of cancer patients. They also began recruiting nurses who could act as "sitters-in," to give relatives who were caring for patients with cancer adequate time for sleep and recreation. Introduced in 1958, the "Day and Night Nursing Service" now employs the services of over two thousand nurses. They are accessible through local Health Departments. In the words of the report—"there are all kinds of attention which the patient requires (at night), including giving nourishment, adjusting the air-ring and pillows, helping him during the hours of restlessness and giving a sedative...." To this one could add the giving of pain-killing injections if they are necessary.

Surveys of state services for the dying usually conclude that they are inadequate, sometimes sadly so.[135, 221] For example, when the family doctor is off duty he will often be replaced by a locum who probably knows nothing of the patient's history. When a patient is discharged from hospital it may be days or weeks before the family doctor is informed. In some areas it may be difficult to find the patient a hospital bed when urgently needed, and all over the country home helps and Meals on Wheels are usually in short supply. Even worse, the services which are available are not co-ordinated.[34] There may be no one connected with the family who is aware of the various available state and voluntary services, and they do not know who to ask.

Men are more often looked after at home than women because many of them can be nursed by their wives. But if an aged husband has to care for his wife, it may prove to be beyond his capabilities though, of course, some manage admirably. The people in the worst plight are those who live alone. They constituted 7% of those mentioned in the Marie Curie Survey, and are likely to suffer great hardship from lack of proper care. However, I do not wish to paint too dismal a picture, because most people who die at home do so with adequate care, and indeed a half of those dying of cancer will never need any difficult nursing.[242] What is needed more than anything else is reassurance and a sense of security. A good family doctor is the key figure in this respect, his frequent visits giving a great boost to morale.[4]

"Do you think he knows?"

The position of the family doctor may be beset by problems. He can at best make a guess as to how long the patient will live (indeed it is well nigh impossible to tell[37, 163]), and yet he has to be firm and decisive. Well-meaning relatives may put pressure on him to follow up every conceivable avenue of treatment, whether appropriate or not, when he knows that staying his hand and allowing a peaceful death would be much kinder to the patient. He may have to discourage more excitable relatives from pursuing all manner of expensive quacks or well-intentioned but ineffectual attempts at cancer cure.

Sometimes a crisis develops because the doctor miscalculates and is too late in transferring the patient to a hospital. This is often because no hospital beds are available in the area.[4, 242] A hospice is the ideal place, but these will not be universally available for a few years yet. Another reason for failing to transfer a patient to hospital is the misguided one of hoping to protect him from realising the gravity of his condition. The result can then be a last minute dash, with the patient *in extremis*, into a hospital where he dies within hours. A coroner's post-mortem often follows this turmoil, adding to the dismay and sense of failure of distressed relatives. It is infinitely more desirable to face up to the situation with the whole family so that panic never develops, and everyone quietly soldiers through at home to the end. This raises the whole vexed question of how and when to tell people of their grave prognoses.

The main reason why this job is shirked is because it is painful to all concerned. The family doctor is usually the most suitable person, if he is a trusted friend. People can put up with a great deal of discomfort if they are confident that those who are caring for them are concerned for their comfort, and respect them as individuals. Endless difficulties arise when a man has been deceived about his diagnosis. If he thinks he should be recovering, he may demand more active treatment when he finds he is getting weaker.[18, 73] He may fail to put his affairs in order, or to consult his priest if he is a religious person.[37] Suggestions of radical treatment may alarm him because he has never really faced the truth, although he probably suspects it. Half the fear of a serious prognosis may be a fear of suffering, sometimes quite bizarre, which can be allayed by reassurance and common sense.[191] If there is no frank discussion, this kind of fear can never be relieved. For the fears will almost certainly be there, made worse by uncertainty.

A doctor has not looked at his patients if he thinks they do not know when they are dying simply because he has not told them. When relatives ask "Do you think he knows?", we can point out that it is unlikely that he has not yet realized. "After all," I have said on occasions, "he's not daft is he?" Surveys in hospitals by Professor Hinton[93] and Dr. Exton-Smith[63] found a much higher proportion of patients with strong suspicions or actual knowledge of their diagnosis than had previously been believed.

There are so many ways that a patient can find out. He may read his hospital notes or overhear chance comments by relatives or doctors, or he may just draw the obvious conclusion when the family rally round, only to avoid him later because of their embarrassment. One girl said to me "I knew it was cancer from the moment they started lying to me."[213] Referral to a radiotherapy unit, or a hospital known to specialize in cancer, is often seen by the patient as a death warrant, and should be discussed with him at once. People will never get to know that cancer can often be cured if they are never allowed to discuss it. Many people have declined to see their doctor with an early cancer because they have thought it might be incurable. All they need is to be assured that this view is now outdated. The Marie Curie Foundation have made this education easier by publishing explanatory leaflets.[129]

When 231 people who were told that they had cancer were followed-up in one survey,[5] only 7% said they would rather not have been told. One in five denied even having been told, which indicates that those not ready to know have a built-in defence against hearing. Certainly no harmful effects were recorded.[50, 107]

Of course a blunt stark thunderbolt is not the only alternative to telling lies. The conversation should be led by the patient. The truth can be given in small doses over several meetings, and then in such a way that it does not hurt.[141] Here are a few examples of how the appropriate words come to mind when the actual situation presents itself :

Miss W. was in a slightly confused state, which added fears of madness to her fear of physical suffering. After several unsuccessful attempts to reassure her I said, "Miss W., you're *all right*. You're

just not immortal." She relaxed and smiled. "Good; I know," she
said, "This is where the story ends."

Mr. T. asked if he had leukaemia, I said "No, nothing so awful
as leukaemia, but trouble in the prostate gland."

"I thought as much," he said.

"Yes, it's acting malignantly, but obviously not very malignantly
as you can see from the length of time you've had it." (Over four
years). He looked relieved and went on to ask about his hearing
aid.

Two days before Mr. V. died we had this conversation, which
said all that was needed without dredging up the hard words:

"They told me there was a shadow in my lung on the X-ray.
What was it?"

"A bit of a growth on this side."

"But they told me there was nothing to worry about."

"There never is."

"Good."

Mr. S. was a patient who wanted to leave everything to us, and
made it plain that he did not want to know his diagnosis. I
accepted this decision, but would not join in his imaginary game
of "when I get better."

"Right," I said, "we'll get that pain of yours under control."

"I'm glad of that. I'm not going to peg out just yet then?"

At first I hesitated (which he did not notice) before replying,
"Not *just* yet."

"Oh good," he said, "I've got a lot of gardening to do."

"Well, I'm not sure you'll be able to do very much of that."

"No, I see. But I'll be able to potter about a bit?"

"We'll have to see how you go over these next few days."

"All right. I'm glad you can do something for me."

"Yes, we'll get rid of that pain."

The point is that you give the patient a choice of directions for
the conversation to take. He will indicate what he is ready to hear.
It is almost like a dance. A man like Mr. S. will come very gradu-
ally round to a fuller realization of his situation, at his own speed.
It is most important that one never takes away all hope,[8] a point
I shall enlarge on in a later chapter.

One patient wrote down for us his experience of being told his
diagnosis of cancer. Here is what he said:

"I had always had a subconscious dread of surgery, so that when I went for the first consultation I was apprehensive to say the least. But the surgeon was so forthright that when an operation was discussed, I felt such complete confidence in him that this banished all sense of fear.

I was admitted to hospital and very soon had the 'exploratory' operation. The following day I was told of the tumour in the gullet and that a major operation was essential. Again, because I was given the details of what was to be done, I felt no fear.

After the immediate post-operative discomfort I still had difficulty with swallowing, and this caused me some depression. However, eventually I began to manage to swallow small quantities of soft food and by the time I was discharged my confidence returned. In the following weeks I appeared to make remarkable strides towards recovery and I began to plan the early return to various activities.

But then I began to feel my strength failing and my ambitions seemed less attractive—depression returned.

Then came the visits from the Out-Patients Sister and the invitation to attend the Clinic. Soon I began to feel a new interest and visits to the Clinic became something to anticipate with real pleasure and the treatment soon brought about improvement.

Meantime a germ of suspicion had been forming in my mind that there might be something more than the weakness following a major operation, and I made some probing observations in the family to see if they were keeping something from me. I learned nothing!

Eventually I made up my mind—I would ask the direct question of the doctor. He had apparently come to a similar conclusion—I was not ready to be told.

I felt no sense of shock nor any fear—the doctor had crystallized my own thoughts and a feeling of calm and relief took the place of the doubt.

I am sure that in my weak and confused condition just after the operation and the depression of the ensuing weeks, it would have been quite wrong to burden my mind with the knowledge that I could not be cured."

After he had been told he was dying, this patient's wife wrote:

"He took it very well—as I knew he would—and I now consider that it was right to wait until he regained his composure, before revealing the facts. We are now able to discuss the future without difficulty and to make arrangements accordingly."

Practical Points

More hints for nursing the dying will be mentioned in the next two chapters, but here are some special hints for home management :

Friends and neighbours often rally wonderfully to the aid of the dying, especially in working-class communities.[114] With their help, relatives may be able to arrange a night rota for attending to the

Strathclyde House Marie Curie Home, Glasgow

patient's nocturnal needs. However, the task is often left to a patient's unmarried daughter, who may have considerable financial difficulty if she has given up her job to undertake the nursing. When a family is having difficulty[201] and showing signs of breakdown, a health visitor or a social worker may be able to approach other relatives for help for which an overburdened spouse was too proud to ask. These workers and the district nurse also know of various aids and sources of helpful equipment. Too often inter-communication between these three professions is hard to establish, unless they are co-ordinated by attachment to a general practice.

The strains to which relationships in a family may be subjected are well summarized in a paper by Alison Player, an Australian social worker.[172] Feelings of guilt and desertion and the resurgence of old family feuds are among the possibilities she lists. Margaret

Birley, another social worker, describes how unfounded fears that cancer may be dirty or infectious or contagious can put up barriers between people.[22]

Relatives can be assisted by various services provided by the Health Department, the British Red Cross Society, Women's Royal Voluntary Services and the District Nursing Association. Different agencies provide the various services in each area. There are usually Meals on Wheels (including special diets for invalids who need them), home helps, an incontinence laundry, nursing equipment, night nurses and special financial grants. The Marie Curie Foundation Information Bureau (01-730 9157) may be able to advise on how to meet the needs of individual patients. Relatives who have to stay with a patient day and night and have already done so for six months, may be entitled to an Attendance Allowance grant. Forms to apply for this are available from the Post Office or Department of Health and Social Security.

Relatives should beware of the temptation to over-protect a patient and to leave him dumped in a chair with nothing to do, completely bypassed by life. The ladies can still plan the meals, control the housekeeping funds and supervise the children for as long as possible. The men should still be accorded the dignity of master of the house. This will avert the development of depression.

District nurses have access to special equipment such as bedpans, commodes, rubber mats and draw-sheets, backrests, inflatable rubber rings for the patient to sit on, and cradles to keep heavy bedclothes off his feet. Some local boroughs also provide ripple beds, though it should not be supposed that these can replace the need for regular two-hourly turning of a patient who is in danger of developing bedsores. Four-hourly turning is adequate at night.

How to turn people, and lift them up the bed, how to care for pressure areas and how to carry out other nursing procedures can all be demonstrated by a district nurse. Although she will do a great deal of heavy nursing, she could not possibly look after a severely ill patient without considerable co-operation from the relatives. However, she can advise and encourage them and warn them what to expect. She may recommend that the more alert patients be taken out if possible, or occupied with hobbies if not. Advice may be needed on managing colostomies (where the bowel is brought to the front of the abdomen because of obstruction in the back passage) which can be washed out with plain water every morning; how to clean and replace the tubes in a tracheostomy (where the windpipe is opened at the front of the throat because its top end is blocked), and how to put liquidized food down a gastrostomy (a tube into the stomach because the gullet is blocked), and all these are the province of a district nurse.

A patient with a tube in the gullet,* which prevents a cancer obstructing the passage of food, will need to be told to keep it disinfected by taking a spoonful of clear honey after any food or drink, to avoid lumps of meat, salad, cabbage and other foods which block the tube, and to clear it with a drink of fizzy lemon if it does block up. For incontinent patients the nurse can show how to make a nappy with towelling, and can provide draw-sheets and incontinence pads to put on the bed. She can demonstrate how to feed people who need it without ramming in too much food and causing regurgitation.

The nurse can help with bedbaths, and enemas when needed, but is unlikely to be present for the last wash, which is usually carried out by the undertakers. Never underestimate undertakers. Their skill and tact constitute the best possible grief therapy, and they guide the relatives gently over any complications during early bereavement. Undertakers can be important members of the team.

Transfer to Hospital

Even with the best home care, hospital admission may eventually be necessary.[178]

Most patients will oppose it, because they will realise what it means : the last look at home, an end to the continuous company of loved ones, and even of pets. Going into hospital is the first stage of dying. Some relatives will see it as a failure on their part, and will need assuring that the admission was unavoidable. Exigencies which may precipitate that move are many; nervous or physical exhaustion of the relative with most of the nursing work, for instance, or the onset of confusion or incontinence in the patient, or symptoms which the family doctor finds he is unable to control.[145, 176] If contact between the hospital and the family doctor has been maintained—by a visiting social worker for instance —then the transfer can be much easier. The social worker can ease the feeling of the relatives that they are "putting their loved one

* e.g. Souttar's or Celestin's tube.

away," and can comfort the patient with the thought that his family will have a rest.[22]

For the relief of all this distress, the ideal would be to have a skilled home care service, on call day and night. Hospices are now beginning to provide this.[134] The service is based on an out-patients clinic to which family doctors can refer patients with pain problems or other symptoms of terminal disease. The clinic advises on drug and similar treatment, and enables the patient to meet others who have, for a while at least, been discharged from the wards with their symptoms under control. When the patient becomes weaker and cannot travel to the clinic, then a doctor or sister, trained in terminal care, visits the home. Should the patient later need to be admitted to the wards, it is to a place he knows and trusts, with staff he has already met.[136]

The clinic works in close co-operation with the family doctors and district nurses, providing visiting nurses with special training in symptomatic treatment, and social workers experienced in listening to the fears and anxieties of this situation. It has been found that if these people go to the patients' homes as friends, rather than in uniform, they can establish a more intimate relationship. The clinic day itself is also a social occasion. One patient attending the clinic at St. Joseph's told a nurse "I stayed in bed all day yesterday to be sure I would be strong enough for Dr. Lamerton's party!" The club-like atmosphere, the visiting of old friends in the wards and the relief of symptoms and anxiety are a tremendous boost to the morale. As a result many patients who would otherwise have needed admission, never come to the wards at all.

Family doctors say how very encouraging it is to be able to tell a patient awaiting admission to the hospice for a terminal condition that there will be no need for him to remain indefinitely as an in-patient: his recovery may justify a return home in the care of the ever-available out-patients staff. They also comment that it is a help to be able to contact the clinic to see if support could be given to patients before the need for admission arises. Not only doctors refer patients: help is sought by their district nurses or medical social workers, and some are introduced by relatives who have heard of the service. But whoever refers the patient, the situation is first discussed with the family doctor. The patient remains in his care, but almost invariably he welcomes this extra help and support for his patients and their families.

St. Luke's Hospital, Bayswater, London

4

Dying in Hospital

PEOPLE may die in hospital from many different diseases[63]—pneumonia or severe bronchitis, heart attacks, heart failure, strokes, thrombosis and gangrene; cancers and leukaemias; tremors and paralyses, arthritis and fractures. Whatever the nature of the illness, there are certain principles to be observed. Before it becomes apparent that the disease is incurable, most of these patients will have undergone some attempt at curative treatment. But once this is abandoned, it will give place to symptomatic treatment. This will involve the whole hospital staff in a complete change of approach. The different concept of "Terminal Care" will govern their actions when a "trial of therapy" as Professor Duncan Vere called it,[228] has failed.

Symptomatic Treatment

When cure is no longer the aim, the staff will use all their skill to bring the patient comfort, treating each symptom as it arises. Many doctors and nurses find this adjustment in aim difficult. A new restraint is now needed in the use of drugs and other life-saving measures. The correct treatment of pneumonia is a case in point :

In the elderly and infirm, bronchopneumonia is not the violent

35

disease with high fever and shortness of breath which we see in a young person. Instead, without causing much distress, it gently induces drowsiness and a peaceful death. The onset of pneumonia is an indication that the patient's body has stopped fighting, and that he is ready to go. Sometimes—by no means always—the patient's condition can be temporarily improved by giving him oxygen, antibiotics, physiotherapy, vitamins and perhaps blood transfusions. The apparent success of this treatment might give the staff a glowing sense of achievement, so there is a great temptation to have a try. But if a man has a cancer which is spreading, or if he is already paralysed and senile from a severe stroke, such interference would be inappropriate, bad, "meddlesome medicine." In these circumstances, the correct treatment for bronchopneumonia is to give the patient an opiate, which suppresses breathlessness and any pain, steroid drugs which relieve the fever and some of the weariness and loss of appetite, and, at the end, a belladonna drug can be added to the narcotic to dry up the secretions in the throat and lungs and ease any feelings of panic.

There are some infections which cause such discomfort that their treatment with antibiotics is expedient, though only for purposes of relief, not of healing. Infections of the bladder, mouth and eyes, and of bedsores are examples. It is not necessary to use drip-feeding into veins, operations like a gastrostomy (p. 33) which merely lengthen the process of dying, or experimental new drugs which have been eagerly advertised.

The doctor has to realign his whole attitude to his patient. First of all he must discover which symptom distresses the patient most. This can be quite a surprise. Constipation may be causing him more concern than his cancer of the face; having a dry mouth may be more burdensome than a growth the size of a football. If pain is present, then drugs must be given in sufficient quantity to control it (p. 47 and 105), and they should be given immediately the patient is admitted to the hospital. This gives him a sense of security from the outset. At all times there must be a pause before active therapy is begun and the question asked : is it really relevant at this time for this patient?

The most drastic test of this rational approach comes on the rare occasions when a patient's cancer bleeds profusely and fatally. All one's training and instinct cry for frantic action. Stop the haemorrhage! There is an urge to rush about and do things. But remembering that, even if it can be stopped now, it will only bleed again and kill him later, one can see that the patient just needs someone to hold on to.[60] Several hospitals keep a large red blanket in a handy cupboard for such occasions. This can soak up the blood without making it obvious, so that the patient is spared the frightening sight of spreading redness. Curtains are quickly pulled round the bed, and someone must sit on the bed as a companion for the person.

The Patient is a Person

Hospital administration can too easily lose sight of the needs of a patient. In one I saw a big graph on the wall comparing different surgeons' statistics of "patient throughput." Empty beds and beds occupied for more than a week by one patient were marked in red, bringing opprobrium on the surgeon concerned, irrespective of the standard of his medicine. Perhaps doctors intent on promotion may think in terms of "cases." The acute ones may be considered more interesting because they are more taxing on the memory and intellect, and may fill a niche in the hunt for more diverse experience. Being usually overworked, nurses often narrow down the sphere of interest they take in the patients, and may answer the question "Which is Mrs. Henderson?" with "She's the breast in bed twenty-two." A "good patient" is one who never complains and quietly fits into the system without question. It follows that a frightened patient who asks questions, or a dignified one who wishes to go on being Mrs. Henderson, will be a nuisance, a "bad patient."

Of course these mistakes are not made everywhere. When they are, it is pointless to criticize the hospital staff for treating people as less than men, when their actions are just a reflection of values throughout modern society. In spite of the strains under which doctors and nurses generally find themselves, however, the special circumstances of dying patients should always call forth respect.

The patient will probably have a suspicion of his diagnosis. Members of the staff may have let hints slip from their lips or actions, and his suspicions and fears can be dreadful. In these circumstances it is essential that he clearly understands who has ultimate responsibility for his case, and that that person spends some time with him.[71, 246] Since there is always something to be done for a patient, it is inexcusable to by-pass his bed on ward rounds even if he is, or seems to be, asleep. Palliative surgery would have to be suggested with utmost discretion and gentleness if it is not to be refused point blank. Even more tact is needed if the patient is sent to die at home or in a hospice when the hospital has no more to offer him and the bed is needed urgently. The significance of the move will probably be obvious, and not helped by sugarcoated lies about "going for convalescence." In the long term his failure to recover will be easier for the patient to bear if he has been warned that he will need nursing care for longer than it can be given in a busy general ward.[196]

The patient should never be made to feel rejected, useless or in the way.[128] He may be greatly helped by his fellow patients, and may in turn support others, by helping them to cope with problems he has already faced. Frequent and, if possible, regular visits from family and friends will be the mainstay of his morale. If they find the visiting painful or embarrassing, it may help for them to be joined for a while by someone less involved, perhaps a nurse, a social worker or a responsible volunteer. The best catalyst of all for facilitating warm interaction between people is the family's new baby. Children should never be excluded from the hospital for fear of frightening them. They can make visiting so much easier, and bring the dying patient an assurance of new life and continuity. It has been our experience that they are not distressed themselves.

Mrs. B., one of my patients who was blind, had just been cuddling her baby grandson. "It's lovely when they're here," she said, "Some of us comes and some of us goes!"

Blocked Beds

Many patients with terminal illnesses cannot be discharged from hospital for one reason or another. In Dr. Exton-Smith's series[63] some 60% of the patients were already bedridden before admission. The longer a patient is in the ward, the less attention he tends to receive from the doctors.[115] The nursing may be heavy, which takes valuable staff away from acutely ill patients. It is easy to regard this as what was called in the *Lancet* a "blocked bed." However, neglect is never justifiable whether the patient is dying or not. Stiff limbs and incontinence are sometimes avoidable by good physiotherapy. If the patient is still keen to be active—even if a little unrealistically—it is a pity to add frustration to all his other troubles.

In severe long-standing illness a weariness and heaviness fills the body and the mind. It can be like an endless feeling of boredom, or the all-over aching and restlessness of flu. For the staleness of mind the best psychotherapy we can offer is listening, while the dullness in the body may be much relieved by physiotherapy.

A patient who has been in bed for a long time may have got out of the habit of moving and walking. This immobility leads to the development of bedsores and stiffness. Over-protective relatives may unwittingly bring this upon a patient by doing too much for him, perhaps because they have been afraid to let him walk about. But there is no point in becoming bedbound before it is inevitable. A patient should walk as long as it pleases him to walk. If it was pain which prevented him from being mobile, then once that has been removed, he can be on his feet again provided he is given a little encouragement.[53,54] The dying may also have many other minor ailments besides their terminal one. These should not be neglected and allowed to cause discomfort. Such complaints as weak leg muscles, stiff necks or low back pain are often amenable to physiotherapy. Patients with pre-existent strokes and paralyses are also helped if their exercises are continued till the last possible day. An essential adjunct to this treatment is regular chiropody.

This is all valuable as long as there is good communication between the doctor and the physiotherapists.[52] Precise decisive instructions are needed as to who is to have his chest kept clear to help breathlessness, and who is to be left in peace. Unless there is understanding between the staff on such matters, one can rehabilitate a patient *too much*. The point is that if physiotherapy helps the person to die comfortably, it is of value.[55] But if the physiotherapist successfully bangs his chest clear of pneumonia, the patient will only have to die of it all over again.

The patient with cancer often has "too much time to think" as Taylor and Michaels have pointed out. In their book[152] they recommended the systematic use of games of all kinds, under the supervision of the occupational therapist.

A vital member of the staff who will usually be of help to a patient who is in the ward for any length of time is the Hospital Chaplain.[126, 248] If he is not included in the caring team (p. 21), then the care is incomplete. Doctor, priest and nurse should work in close collaboration round the bed of a dying patient.[74, 187] For however ill, however confused, he is still a whole person in need of care. Never should the names "vegetable" or "cabbage" or "the

39

breast in bed twenty-two" be used even for the remains of a human person. Use of such names betrays ignorance and refusal to look.

The Family in the Hospital

The death of a person should leave his family with no regrettable memories.

They should be involved in his care as surely as they would be if he were at home. They can help the nurses with feeding him, turning him, washing him and so on. As this is their last offering to him, they want to be as intimately close to him as possible. Think of the person you most love, and then imagine having to say goodbye from a distance.

If visiting is proving too expensive for the family, the social worker may be able to get money to help with fares from such charities as the National Society for Cancer Relief.* She can also help them with their feelings of guilt at having failed to go on caring for the patient at home. If he returns to their care for a while, the hospital consultant's continued interest can be confirmed by visits from the social worker. She can help to arrange hospice admission or convalescence, as well as informing the consultant when the patient needs readmission if the family are having difficulties. Often a patient will not accept his invalid state until he has tried a period at home and found for himself that he cannot manage. For cancer patients who need heavy nursing it may be possible to secure a holiday in the nearest Marie Curie Home, to give the relatives a rest. Margaret Bailey recommends a holiday together for the whole family while the patient is still strong enough.[15]

The social worker has to resist the temptation to avoid the patient by concentrating on helping the relatives. In a hospital she may be the only person with the time to sit and listen to him, and as she is the "lay" member of the team, some patients may find it easier to talk to her than to the doctors or the nurses.[149]

These families will take priority on the services of the social worker, because of the short time limit involved. Often her prime duty will be to help them to face up to their imminent bereavement, and later they may need help with handling funerals, estates, and grief.

While the patient is in hospital, someone will have to keep the

* 2, Cheam Court, Cheam, Surrey.

relatives informed of his progress and expectations. This task is commonly delegated to the houseman or ward sister and can be difficult because the hospital staff do not usually know the family very well. If no real relationship has been established, it is always worth considering whether the family doctor is not a much better person to break hard news to the family particularly as he is then available for follow-up.[74] The best use can be made of this relationship if the doctor has his own beds in a local cottage hospital.[114, 176]

News of the imminent death of a patient can be as hard for his relatives to accept as it is for the patient himself. I was recently asked by Mrs. H., whose husband had bowel cancer, "There isn't anything to worry about is there doctor?" I decided to break the news to them gently, in stages, and parried the question by saying "Not really, but of course the colostomy (p. 109) will be permanent now." The next time I saw her I told her that he would have to have the fluid drawn off from his tummy frequently for quite a long time "because the irritation is still there." With each new piece of information she expressed surprise and consternation. Then my partner returned from holiday and told me he had already taken Mrs. H. through this process once, and had told her his diagnosis before going on holiday!

Little of the first interview will be assimilated. A common reaction is to plead that the patient should not be told. But more than once I have been asked by a patient not to distress his wife with such news, while at the same time the wife has been asking me to conceal the diagnosis from her husband. If the situation where only one of a couple has been informed should arise, then the other may later ask what the doctor said. I have helped several people in this predicament by returning with them to the patient's bed and saying something like "Hello, Mr. Heath, your wife has just been helping me to fill up your forms, and she tells me you are interested in sailing . . ." etc.

When the patient does die, his family may again find the fact hard to accept. It helps if they can have been present and seen that the end was peaceful. Dr. Cicely Saunders points out that to have said goodbye can be a great consolation, especially if it can be said that "Last time he woke up, you were the last person he saw."

A helpful little ritual impinges itself here : the doctor has to hand over the death certificate, which gives the relatives something to do. They have to take the certificate (page 80) by hand to the

Registrar of Births and Deaths whose office is usually in the Town Hall. An undertaker then has to be contacted and told whether burial or cremation is preferred—he will do the rest. Cremation is the commonest method of disposal, and costs less than burial. People rarely ask for embalming nowadays.

The family can be asked if the patient would have liked to give the corneas of his eyes for a surgeon to graft on to someone else. Only a doctor or nurse who has become a friend of the family, and who was seen to give tender caring to the patient before he died, is in a position to make this request, however. Relatives should be reassured that this will not disfigure the body. Neither this nor a post-mortem should be requested lightly by someone who has not earned the family's respect. If other organs are wanted for transplanting, then it is the consultant's duty to ask for them. To deal with this particular exigency, ethical codes are being developed in all countries to ensure that the patient's death is confirmed by an independent doctor not associated with the transplanting surgeon.

Finally the hospital staff should mobilize community services for the after-care of the relatives, a duty which often goes by default. When someone dies in hospital his family doctor in particular should be informed the same day.

I hope I have made it evident that there is often room for improvement in the care of the dying in hospitals. With Dame Albertine Winner,[246] I can only chorus :

"When all is said and done, it is good doctoring and good nursing that is needed more than anything else, so why don't we give it?"

The Hostel of God Clapham, London

5

How Hospices Cope

THE word "hospice" is reminiscent of the Middle Ages when hundreds of hospices were dotted all over Europe, where travellers found food, refuge and spiritual encouragement to fit them for the journey ahead. Mary Aikenhead applied this name to terminal hospitals because she saw them as fulfilling a parallel purpose, death to her being a thoroughfare, not a terminus.

For many years nuns and other Christian groups have run terminal homes on both sides of the Atlantic, and in 1952 the Marie Curie Foundation opened the first of its homes. It should be pointed out that in these homes, as well as caring for people dying of cancer, they also rehabilitate patients whose cancers have been cured. With 410 beds in 12 homes this is the largest voluntary organization in the field. Within the National Health Service are St. Luke's, Bayswater and St. Columba's, Hampstead. Most of the hospices, however, are independent charities, often working with support from the Department of Health and Social Security, though the Hostel of God in Clapham is completely independent of State support.

History

To St. Luke's Hospital and St. Joseph's Hospice, Hackney, goes the honour of being the first to put the care of the dying on a firm scientific footing. In the nineteen fifties purpose-built wards were opened at St. Joseph's. The building has bays of six beds with a spacious central day-room. As the windows reach almost to the floor, a patient in bed can see across the gardens and into a busy thoroughfare. Consequently he is not cut off from day to day events, but can still enjoy the turmoil of the traffic and fire engines and fights of the East End in which he has always lived. To put someone in a window bed is the best cure for depression at St. Joseph's. In contrast to this, patients at Ardenlea Marie Curie Home in Ilkley told me how wonderful it was to look out over their beloved Yorkshire Moors.

Hospices usually provide room for visitors to stay all day, so that they can share in looking after the patients if they wish to. Gardens are a great asset, especially if the patients' beds can be wheeled into them. In the wards, the televisions are silent with lightweight earphones on every bed for any patient who wants to listen.[194]

Earlier in this century hospices were mainly concerned with people dying of tuberculosis, but now cancer holds the stage. Indeed the Marie Curie Homes are exclusively for cancer patients. The Irish Sisters of Charity have hospices in Eire, Britain and Australia. Other recent foundations not run by religious orders are in New Haven, U.S.A.; Manchester, Brighton, Thornton, Sheffield, Worthing and Stoke in Britain; and Kalorama in Holland. Jospice International has several homes in S. America and Pakistan. The idea is meeting with enthusiasm everywhere, and those who are planning new hospices are turning to those already established.

From the outset Mary Aikenhead linked the care of dying patients in the wards with community care and the support of the sick in their homes. This lady's genius set the pattern which the new hospices are still adopting today.

Most of these institutions are religious in essence, working in close co-operation with the clergy of all faiths. All have a remarkably peaceful and—dare I say it?—distinctly joyful atmosphere. They are thus establishing a rather different reputation from the municipal homes for the elderly described by Peter Townsend.[221] Many of these are grim ex-workhouses where regimentation drains away the individuality and happiness of the inmates. As Professor Hinton said in his Pelican book *Dying,*

"To choose between a below-standard hospital for the chronic sick and a poor home is a painful dilemma. Many dying people or their relatives have to do this, some in ignorance and some with painful awareness of the implications."

The opening of hospices in every community will make available to all men as they die the benefit of the skills and experience now being developed.

Let us examine some of these skills more closely.

Teaching

Care of the dying is best learnt by practice. A film or lecture can be stimulating, but it is no substitute for personal experience. For this reason hospices welcome visits from groups of students, nurses and anyone else who is professionally interested. Ward rounds and discussions are useful, but it may be more helpful for a student to be introduced to the patient and left to see what he can learn from this encounter. From the patient's point of view another interested visitor is usually welcome; and for the student—here is life in all its unpredictable wonder. Such a breath of fresh air after all the books!

These ward rounds are becoming more popular as a gap in medical education is recognized. Medical students in Sheffield receive instruction in St. Luke's Home[243] and in Sydenham St. Christopher's Hospice now has a new teaching centre, where individual tutorials and small discussion groups are the mainstay of the teaching. Medical students and ordinands do holiday work and gain valuable first hand experience in the wards of both these hospices. As more hospices open it is this—more than any theoretical teaching—which will bring up a new generation able and ready to cope with proper care of the dying both in general hospitals and in their own homes.

There is also a duty to educate the general public. Books, articles,[83] letters in newspapers[211] and hospice open days[108] all contribute to help the community to a calmer, less fearful approach to dying. Soon people will cease to associate serious illness and death with inevitable pain, but rather will actually expect to have a joyful death. The Marie Curie Foundation publishes an excellent series of leaflets to educate the public on the prophylaxis and management of cancer, stressing the high proportion of cures now possible.

Medical Skills

The principles of symptomatic treatment with drugs are simple. The first secret lies in realising that when we give people drugs, it is not like feeding data into a machine. People respond differently to any one drug. And the second secret is that symptoms should be anticipated.

Why should patients with terminal illness—notably cancer—have to suffer so much pain when the knowledge of effective pain control is now so widespread? While many doctors may have encountered a confounding case where nothing they could do with drugs, surgery or radiation, was able to control the pain, such cases are very rare. Usually all that is required is someone who cares enough.[128] Caring is such an effort, isn't it? In an age of disposable everythings, "just heat and eat," "labour saver—just spray it on," taking care is less and less exercised, and becomes unfashionable.

One sometimes hears odd comments about pain which prompt doubts about our whole way of life :

"All right, I'll let Doctor know it's hurting again, but we just have to bath you now."

"Mr. Smith keeps saying he's in pain, but I doubt it : he's always demanding attention."

You can tell if a man is in pain simply by looking and listening. A wrinkled brow, tense fingers and cautious breathing may betray underlying pain even in an unresponsive patient. It has been noted that these signs can even be removed in some unconscious patients by the administration of analgesics. But in order to notice these signs, and to feel inclined to do something about them, it is necessary really to look, and to care.

Each kind of pain has its distinctive treatment. For minor pains there are many effective agents, particularly variations on the aspirin theme. These may be sufficient by themselves, but if they do not control pain adequately, one can progress to a number of more powerful drugs which are available as tablets (Fortral, Dieconal and Narphen are popular examples). For severe pain, however, the strong narcotic analgesics may eventually be needed(for example morphine, diamorphine and physeptone). Fearing that the patient might become addicted, doctors are often reluctant to use adequate doses of these drugs. Given by mouth, often mixed with a little gin and cocaine in one of the variations of the so-called "Brompton cocktail," these drugs do not have to be given in the ever-increasing doses dreaded by those unaccustomed to their use. Of course, if an inadequate dose is given, by injection, so that by the time of the next medicine-round the patient has pain again and is longing for the relief that the injection brings, then the scene is perfectly set for the development of physical and psychological dependence.

Most people can cope with short-term pain, but what we most fear is pain which lasts for months. This constant pain will need constant control with analgesics, and if the control is to be sustained the drug must obviously be given regularly, day and night. Pain severe enough to require large doses of narcotics is rare. The usual starting dose in one hospice which uses diamorphine is five or ten milligrams, given by mouth every four hours. This may be increased, to reach double that dose before the patient dies. In one series, only 13% of patients ever needed more than a thirty milligram dose, which is a small quantity by any standards. If tolerance (a lessening of effectiveness of the drug because the patient's body is compensating for it) is developing, then there is a substance called amiphenazole (Daptazole) which appears to arrest the process.

It should, however, be noted that for a dying man there is no maximum dose of a pain-killer. If his pain really needs five times the normal quantity (presumably because some measure of tolerance is present) then that is his correct dose. The severer pains may need injections to keep them below the horizon. When they are given by injection, the actual dose of narcotic analgesics should be halved, not kept the same as when given by mouth, because not all of the drug is absorbed from the gut. In short, by carefully observing the individual's response, the doctor can *titrate* his drugs against the patient's pain.[190]

It has been suggested that larger doses of narcotics, because of their inhibitory effect on a patient's breathing, may shorten his life. My experience has been quite the contrary. By easing the sense of breathlessness as well as the pain, these drugs relieve the distress which can exhaust the dying. Being able to rest, they live longer if anything. The popular idea is an utter myth.

Excitement or depression also contribute to pain, perhaps by lowering a man's resistance—his "pain threshold" as the physiologist calls it, and so tranquilizers and anti-depressants have their place in pain relief. For not all pain is physical. . . .

Continuing for a while, however, to consider the physical methods of easing pain, there are many other techniques in the

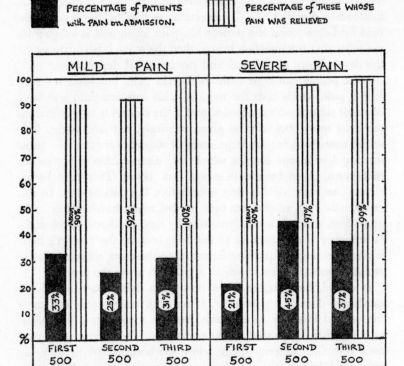

PERCENTAGE of PATIENTS with PAIN on ADMISSION.

PERCENTAGE of THESE WHOSE PAIN WAS RELIEVED

Figure A. Pain relief: the record of one hospice.

doctor's arsenal. Gardham wrote a paper, for instance, on the use of surgery just for the relief of symptoms, without hoping to effect a cure.[70] The neurosurgeon may be able to help by cutting the pain-carrying nerves, or the anaesthetist by paralysing them. Radiotherapy may cause shrinkage of large tumours which are exerting painful pressure on surrounding parts of the body, and so may some hormones and "cytotoxic" drugs. The ingenuity of modern medicine is quite wonderful, but as death approaches, many of these techniques give steadily diminishing returns. Most of them anyway, may have unpleasant side-effects. There comes a time when these measures should neither be initiated nor continued. All that is necessary is that the doctor should pause and ask himself Sir Stanford Cade's famous question "What is the relative value of the various available forms of treatment *in this particular patient?*"[36]

Vomiting can usually be controlled by anti-emetic drugs and it is worthwhile to try several different ones to see which works for the patient without making him drowsy. If vomiting is due to an actual blockage of the stomach or bowel (which is rare), then a stomach tube can be passed through the nose to suck out the contents of the stomach before they are vomited. Thereafter his fluid intake will have to be by rectal infusions, with ice lollies to suck to keep his mouth moist. Such use of tubes is very seldom indicated, but when these very unusual circumstances arise, they can bring comfort to the patient. They are not intended to extend his life.

Hiccups usually stop if carbon dioxide is inhaled, so the patient should be told to breath in and out of a paper bag for a few minutes. If this measure fails, an injection of chlorpromazine (Largactil) may help.

Inevitably the doctor will be using a number of different drugs—one for each symptom—and their use should be explained to the patient.

"Did the tablet help your breathing?"

"Oh, I thought it was for the bowels." No comment.

It may be necessary to experiment with different remedies to find what suits each patient, but each doctor gradually fills his box of tricks. Drugs for headaches, nausea, anxiety, loss of appetite,[226] breathlessness, diarrhoea, constipation, coughs and cramps. The list is endless. And drugs are not all. Raising the head or foot of the bed, draining off excesses of fluid collecting in the body cavities or bladder, or pumping fluid away from a swollen hand or leg, can all be of help to some patients. Honey taken after food can stop the unpleasant water-brash in people with cancer of the gullet, and can be used to disinfect bedsores. Oxygen may, rarely, help breathlessness though open windows are better. Alcohol helps almost everything.

Not least, the doctor's own confidence in his remedies can be transmitted to the patient. Nowadays he can meet his patients with the assurance that he can bring comfort. Why, even the "death rattle" itself can be quietened by an injection of a mixture of belladonna and a narcotic. It is due to secretions in the throat which a dying person cannot cough up, and drugs of the belladonna family dry up the production of these secretions.

Certainly our drugs are marvellous, and great fun, but their use is only chemistry at best, and the physics and chemistry are only the deadest part of a man. To know which drugs are needed and which are not, and to know how to relieve distress, we need to look at the patient, and to care. Used in the right way and by those who retain their sensitivity to pain and discomfort, they will be of immense help in the last stages of life.

Nursing Skills

Some aspects of nursing are intensified in caring for the dying, and some fade into the background.[233] There arises, quite naturally, a certain reverence for the patients. This includes unresponsive patients, who must always be handled gently, and treated as if fully aware. Careless conversations over an apparently unconscious person are sometimes clearly heard by that person. It is usually considered that hearing is the last of the senses to fade, and many religions have accordingly provided special prayers to be read quietly into the ear of the dying man.

Routine procedures such as taking the temperature and pulse need not disturb the patient now as they are of no further practical use. On the other hand, attention to the patient's appearance preserves his dignity. The men should still be shaved regularly, and the ladies should have their hair done.

When a new patient arrives at a hospice he is welcomed by name while still in the ambulance, and his future ward sister or staff nurse accompanies him to the ward. It is important that the relatives should also be welcomed, because henceforth treatment will be directed towards the whole family. Suffering will not be confined to the patient himself : everyone who loves him will to some extent be a patient of the hospice.

When his pain is controlled, the patient may be well enough to get up, or even to go home for a few weeks. Many will spend part of the morning in the dayroom where they may watch television, develop a new skill in occupational therapy or chat with friends. One hospice has a sitting room in which patients who are mobile enough can entertain their friends and take tea provided by voluntary workers.

All the ancillary aid possible must be maintained for the patients at this stage,[55] as I will discuss in the next section of this chapter. But as time passes the patient will feel weaker and will want to spend more time in bed, needing ever more intensive nursing. This can be very heavy work for the nurses, and the full complement of nurses to a ward should be the same as for an acute medical ward —namely at least one nurse to one patient* quite apart from ward orderlies and voluntary workers.

It is at this stage that the work of the nurse earns profound admiration. Gradually she has to take over more and more of the patient's activities for him. He will have to be lifted and turned, washed and fed, and all without impinging on his dignity. One girl who recently died of motor neurone disease, and whose only means of communication was by blinking in Morse Code, dictated the following to a friend :

"Possibly I am particularly sensitive, but I hate to be fed. Nevertheless it makes an enormous difference to one's enjoyment of a meal if the person helping takes a real interest in what she is doing. I know that it must require infinite patience, but there are some people who will go to endless trouble to keep the food hot, and make it as tasty as possible. They also give the impression that there is nothing they would rather be doing at that particular time. Others, however, will carry on an animated conversation with another, whilst holding an appetising forkful—just out of reach!—or stare out of the window, in deep thought, while one watches the food getting cold.

"The person in whom I have most confidence is the one who goes about her work slowly and deliberately, telling what she is about to do, giving me the opportunity to indicate if anything is wrong. She seems to get through her work just as quickly as the one who exercises a more forceful approach."

The rest of this essay is equally valuable reading, particularly for nurses or physiotherapists.[146]

Our techniques must be good, but we must also give ourselves to the patients. It can be very lonely in hospital, and no amount of science will alleviate that. But one gentle cheerful nurse can. She need not be a Socrates—it is not the profundity of her understanding which is of value—but the fact that she cares enough to try. A nurse who was dying wrote about this as follows :

"I know, you feel insecure, don't know what to say, don't know what to do. But please believe me, if you care, you can't go wrong.

* i.e. including day and night nurses, on or off duty.

Just admit that you care. That is really for what we search. We may ask for why's and wherefores, but we don't really expect answers. Don't run away . . . wait . . . all I want to know is that there will be someone to hold my hand when I need it. I am afraid. Death may get to be a routine to you, but it is new to me. You may not see me as unique, but I've never died before, to me, once is pretty unique!

"You whisper about my youth, but when one is dying, is he really so young any more? I have lots I wish we could talk about. It really would not take much of your time because you are in here quite a bit anyway.

"If only we could be honest, both admit our fears, touch one another. If you really care, would you lose so much of your valuable professionalism if you even cried with me? Just person to person? Then, it might not be so hard to die . . . in a hospital . . . with friends close by."[12]

A number of techniques and methods have been developed in hospices which are worth describing because they may be used at home or in hospital, and bring great relief.

Medicines must be given regularly, every four hours being the best timing, day and night. They should never be inaccessible, for once a patient needs help, there should be no delay. The senior nurses often exercise discretion with drugs. Pain killers and tranquillizers, for instance, are prescribed with a range of doses. The sister can then give the exactly appropriate quantity herself, and thus learn to use the drugs accurately.

Many different methods can be used for avoiding bedsores, but if they do occur this is not a sign of bad nursing—they may sometimes be inevitable. Then one must try at least to render them painless. They arise because of continuous pressure on one patch of the skin of a patient who cannot move about, the places to watch being the heels and base of the spine.

Ripple mattresses with inflatable ribs which are alternately filled and deflated by an electric pump can help by shifting the points on which the person's weight is borne. Some Local Authorities have these for hire. For a slightly mobile patient who is not incontinent, a sheepskin can help to spread the weight. The usual method is just to turn the patient regularly from one side to the other. With this method one should watch that sores do not develop on the hips, and that the sheet does not rub against the skin as the person is being turned. This procedure should be repeated every two to four hours. This need only continue throughout the night if the patient is very sore. All lumps and wrinkles should be smoothed out of the bedding under the patient. If the pressure areas become red, the skin should be gently massaged with a mixture of surgical spirit and olive oil, or just powdered to keep it dry. When a patient is incontinent there should be a rubber or plastic drawsheet, covered by a twill one which can be moved or changed when soiled. Every time this sheet is changed, a barrier cream should be applied to the affected area.

If the skin breaks in spite of all these measures, the sore should be dressed with a disinfectant and a local anaesthetic cream. Cicatrin powder or honey are excellent disinfectants to use. When any slough forming in the floor of the ulcer has been removed, the cavity should be cleaned with hydrogen peroxide ten volumes solution which produces an oxygen-rich foam, killing gangrene germs. (Care should be taken not to splash this solution in the eyes.) The edges of the sore should be gently massaged. Some doctors find that zinc sulphate capsules (220 milligrams, thrice daily) help healing to take place provided they do not cause vomiting. Deep bedsores should be packed with gauze soaked in Eusol and paraffin every six hours to keep them free from infection. Many other forms of treatment are favoured in different hospitals, but the one I have described could also be carried out at home.

To prevent the skin of an incontinent patient becoming soggy it is always worth while to insert a catheter which drains urine from the bladder into a bag. Infection of a catheter can be prevented by a once-weekly dose of a long-acting sulphonamide tablet or some similar drug. If he is still mobile, the patient could have the urine bag strapped to his leg, suspended from his pyjama cord under the dressing-gown or, for the ladies, carried in a little crocheted hand-bag. Male patients who are not confused can use a condom attachment for the urine tube. One of the best is a Stille Uridom, held on with Warne skin adhesive.

Adequate care of the mouth is essential. It pays to have ill-fitting dentures refashioned as long as the person can eat. Chewing gum may freshen up the mouth and help the patient to make saliva.[155] Thrush in the mouth—like flecks of milk curd stuck to the gums and palate, each surrounded by a red inflamed flare—is a constant nuisance to debilitated patients. It is important to be on the lookout for this, because it is extremely uncomfortable but easy to treat. When a patient becomes very weak, mouthwashes every four hours are essential. The mouth may drop open and become dry. Water should be given in frequent small quantities as long as the person can swallow. A gauze wick with one end in ice water and the other in the mouth for the patient to suck has been recommended. Ice wrapped in gauze may be placed inside the cheek to melt gradually, replacing saliva. On the other hand if there is too much saliva, it may be absorbed by wads of gauze placed between the cheek and gums. The patient should be turned on his side so that fluid does not trickle down his windpipe making him cough.

A considerable problem—indeed one of the greatest—is constipation, especially when pain-killing drugs are in use. If laxatives do not work, suppositories may, and an enema may be tried on the third or fourth day. It is worth while to proceed quickly to the most active measures because they make the person feel so much better. A good intake of drinks is a great help, and the motions can be softened by medicines like "Dioctyl." Sometimes bowel blockage produces distension. The doctor can deflate this, for a dying patient, by puncturing the distended loop of bowel with a large hypodermic needle and letting out the gas. The procedure is painless.

If his breathing is laboured, the patient should be turned slightly on his side, and propped up on pillows with his head well supported. To prevent him sliding back down, a "bed donkey" can be inserted on which to rest his feet. A cushion rolled in a sheet which is tucked in at both sides of the bed will do.

Moving an unconscious or semi-conscious person who cannot co-operate is a job for two people, one on each side, linking their hands under him and co-ordinating their efforts by saying "one, two, three, Lift." This requires knowledge of exactly where to place the hands and how to grasp the wrists of the other helper. When the balance and position are exactly right, even heavy people are easy to move. This technique cannot be taught, it comes from practice, bearing in mind the comfort of the patient.[128] Full attention is required, so social conversation at the time should be avoided.

Above all, a dying man needs company. There is usually nothing to do but hold his hand. Hospices have a rule that no one shall die alone : if no relatives can be present, then a nurse or any other sympathetic helper should be with him, day or night.

Other skills

Once a patient has been declared incurable, those not accustomed to treating the dying tend to forget him, to withdraw quickly and leave him alone. The sense of desolation and loneliness to which this often gives rise has been called a state of being "socially dead."[140] The patient becomes depressed and introverted. He may exhibit resentment and aggression, or just an overwhelming hopelessness. He sleeps most of the time, withdrawing from the world into a dark and haunted cavern of dreams and drifting imaginings. This is real suffering.

Holme Tower Marie Curie Home, Penarth, Glamorgan

At this point, the more members of the team who can be interested in the patient, the better.[52] Of course, later on when he is moribund, the need is for the more discreet presence of only one or two trusted friends in an atmosphere of peace and confidence. But as long as the patient can be encouraged to be bright and alert, the less he will suffer. What hope has morphia if the patient is not happy?

One expects to find social workers, physiotherapists, occupational therapists and chaplains in the hospice setting; but also important are the visiting dentist and optician, the family doctor who visits to show he is still concerned, the chiropodist and the hairdresser. Voluntary workers of all kinds can bring their own special abilities and listening ears. They can help in the wards, run the patients' libraries, mobile shops and social functions, as well as launch fundraising programmes.

Patients and Staff

The magic in life springs from our relationships with other people. In a hospice which cares for the dying what happens to the patient's outlook? What happens to the staff?

So often I have heard it said "Terminal care? I couldn't do that, it must be awfully depressing." That this popular picture of a hospice as a gloomy house full of agonized corpse-like people is not accurate, is a tribute to the quality of the nursing. Although extreme illness is treated with horror and people avoid even looking at it,[105] it is often a positive force, binding people together and bringing out the best in them.[119] It is not a question of getting hardened to suffering—one always remains vulnerable. If one person is to receive comfort, someone else has to give it up. Merely staying beside someone who is struggling with physical deterioration and mental anguish can be very painful. But this pain can be a rewarding experience, because of the comfort such fellowship brings to the patient. Although some patients are in the hospice for only a few days, others may spend much longer in the ward. To benefit fully from the care a hospice gives, some patients need to be there for several weeks. Inevitably the staff will make friends with them, so that a series of bereavements for the staff cannot be avoided. If a much loved patient dies, there is a cloud over the whole ward for a while. To support the staff and to develop their own insight, group meetings are held to discuss these matters. For one person alone it might well prove too much, but with the strength of a whole caring community, it is easy. This is the main reason why specialist hospices are needed : the individual's confidence can be sustained by the group which will also guide his attitude to his work.

The patient's hope of recovery should never be completely extinguished. He should never be spoken of as if he were as good as dead, nor should a wholly pessimistic prognosis be given. The staff should always remember that miracles do happen—as I shall recount in a later chapter—in fact, the miraculous is quite commonplace.

I had the honour of helping to care for a lady whose story illustrates several of these points : When she arrived in February Mrs. P. said her cancer had been cured, so she could not think what was wrong with her breast now. She turned off completely, keeping the curtains shut and the bed covers over her head. Having told the psychiatrist that she should have died long ago, she dismissed him by saying she found it hard to open up to people. Gradually Mrs. P.'s depression lifted, and by April she was able to discuss her family problems at length with the doctors and became much easier to nurse. Though she still produced many untreatable symptoms and vague complaints, she did so with a perverse impishness which betrayed growing insight. Occasionally her barriers fell away, and one day she met the psychiatrist with "You don't think you are going to beat me, do you?" He replied, "I thought we were both on the same side." After a brief tirade she suddenly smiled mischievously and squeezed his hand. By June she was able to ask the doctor "Am I dying? Now come on, be honest." She then asked him to read her notes to her, showing much interest, but no distress. When she died, the nurses had all grown very fond of her.

To watch someone coming to terms, in his own special way, with an unbearable situation, is a very great privilege. Here more than anywhere else a good nurse can give valuable help. On their death beds many men mature wonderfully. Priorities fall into place, tolerance and courage may grow in the most unlikely soil and more amazing still is the serenity which so often comes to one from the dying.

Much of the work of those caring for the dying is to prevent anything arising which may hinder this growth in the patient's being. He must be free from pain, but still alert; he must be told as much of the truth about his condition as he can cope with, but no more; he must be encouraged to turn his attention away from himself, and must be given a clean example of real service.[154]

When a man's responsibilities drop away, either by reason of physical weakness or of senile dementia, there remains a great beauty which has been covered by busy-ness—or laziness—for many a year. Death removes the covers: this unmasking can be a thrilling revelation.

When people say that they would find the care of the dying depressing, I wonder whether they are not denying expression to that very part of their nature which could give the most to others. Nurses or doctors who get elated or depressed with their patients are not considering what the patients may need from them. It follows that such feelings must be self-centred. This kind of "involvement" may well render a person useless. For instance, a nurse who vomits when cleaning up an incontinent patient has all her attention on herself, instead of on the needs of the patient. Just so she who grieves with him, suffers with him, "feels for him" or does anything but serve him.[133]

To see a man's needs and to minister to them efficiently and considerately requires a measure of detachment. This is not—as is commonly supposed—a cold thing. Far from it!—it is an indispensable pre-requisite of love. Surges of emotion take your attention off the person in need on to yourself. However, if some situation is very moving another trap is to try to conceal your feelings. When you consider it, such suppression is untruthful. It is better to keep a level head if you can, but if you cannot, at least do not be dishonest about it!

I remember one family who were overwhelmed with gratitude because the nurse who imparted bad news to them also cried with them. "How wonderful," they said afterwards, "that she cared so much." The significant thing, however, was that she *stayed* with them in spite of her own sorrow and embarrassment.

This love is essential in caring for the dying. In a general ward, there is usually so much one can do for the patients[109] that the duty to be with them and the pure giving entailed in listening to them, can be dismissed as an encumbrance. But to provide the dying with masses of hospital equipment and drugs, and no love, is like offering a pot of gold to a starving man buried in sovereigns.

The right attitude to the dying, then, is neither that of a vivisector, nor that of an indulgent granny, but is one of esteem, of reverence, of loving kindness. This is a tall order, certainly, but it is a worthy aim. In this setting one hopes the patient may be able to approach death like the Chinese poet Po Chü-i, who wrote:

> Within my breast no sorrows can abide,
> I feel the great world's spirit through me thrill
> And as a cloud I drift before the wind,
> Or with the random swallow take my will.
>
> As underneath the mulberry tree I dream,
> The water-clock drips on, and dawn appears:
> A new day shines o'er wrinkles and white hair,
> The symbols of the fullness of my years.

If I depart, I cast no look behind;
If still alive, I still am free from care.
Since life and death in cycles come and go,
Of little moment are the days to spare.

Thus strong in faith I wait and long to be
One with the pulsings of Eternity.
Poems transcribed by L. Cranmer-Byng.[76]

The Patient Dies

The vigil of relatives and friends, or just one of the hospice staff, must be discreetly supervised to prevent its being a traumatic experience. People feel helpless beside the dying because they do not realize that what counts is their presence, not their activity. They may feel guilty because the mind plays with irrelevant thoughts, taking attention off the dying person. They should be encouraged to touch the patient—hold his hand for instance—for this will be one of his last channels of reassurance. To the last he can be assumed to hear all that is said. Often a flicker of a smile or a faint squeeze of a finger will confirm that the message has been received. In searching for the appropriate message, people commonly turn to the traditional prayers and scriptures of the Church; the *Nunc Dimittis* for instance :

> Lord, now lettest thou thy servant depart in peace, according to thy word : For mine eyes have seen thy salvation, which thou has prepared before the face of all people.

Luke 2 :29–31.

Distress in the last hour is rare and the fear of it is a morbid twist in our culture. The idea of suffering may well be projected on to a person by distressed spectators who are in fact dreading their own imminent bereavement. There is, on the contrary, almost always a rather beautiful giving-in. The person withdraws serenely and willingly, as gently as an ocean liner slips away from the quayside. Sometimes there may be a brief period of complete lucidity, as in the case of Mr. B. who, when I went to say good-bye, suddenly opened his eyes and said to me "I'm joining your flock now, Doctor. I hope the coffin is ready. Cheerio!"

In the last few hours dying patients will usually prefer being somewhat propped up, with the head well supported to the side. Restlessness probably indicates discomfort so they should be moved frequently but gently. They dislike feeling closed in, so bedclothes should be kept to a minimum. Sunlight, fresh air and flowers are needed. Profuse sweating often occurs necessitating sponging them down and changing the bedclothes. Cold and clammy hands and feet do not usually mean that the patient feels cold. The nostrils can be kept moist and free from crusts with vaseline, and if the mouth is very dry a little fluid can be given in a medicine dropper. More than this will make them choke. In her booklet *Care of the Dying* (see bibliography), Dr. Cicely Saunders wrote,

> "Some have said to me that they hoped 'it would be in their sleep', and this is something we can promise with little fear that we will be wrong. We must be ready to use sedation for the occasional patient who feels that he is choking or suffocating but almost always unconsciousness precedes death."

Even if a body is dead, it is still the most magnificent set of tools yet to have arisen on this earth. And this is not the only reason why it is worthy of respect, for it is still the symbol of a man. His loved ones will refer to it as if it were still the person. When the idea of a post-mortem examination is mentioned by the doctor, his request is often met with a look of anguish and a question such as "Does that mean they'll cut him open?" "Haven't they messed him about enough?" or "Please let him rest now : I don't want that." For this reason academic interest is not, in my view, an adequate excuse for an autopsy[156] and coroners also might stay their hand whenever no obvious benefit will be gained.

Whatever we do outwardly, it is the *inner* respect that matters. I asked a nurse to tell me about the last washing of a body, and what she wrote shows this respect very clearly :

> "To nurse the dying was for me one of the most rewarding types of nursing. I was afraid of death when I first began and therefore chose to do orthopaedic nursing to avoid meeting it. In my general training hospital we were gently introduced to death. If a patient died, an experienced senior nurse would take a junior and teach her very gently how to do the last wash. The atmosphere of the room, the beauty of the ritual and reverence

of the washing and the Presence in the room, removed from me this fear of death.

"The last wash was done in two parts, and between the two parts the priest came and said some prayers. At first when I became attached to a patient who was dying, I did not want to be there to see him die or to perform the last wash, but later it was the opposite. To be able to perform that last act of service was important to me and when I became the senior nurse I was very careful to be gentle with the new junior who was meeting death for the first time."

Conrad House Marie Curie Home, Newcastle-upon-Tyne

6

Dying Children

ONLY two in a hundred U.K. babies die in the first year of life. Most of these deaths will be in the first few hours as a result of congenital disease or obstetrical difficulties. Thereafter, nine out of ten of them will live past their fiftieth birthday. In all, some twenty-seven thousand children die in Britain each year. For centuries the death of children was part of family life, but is now a rarity in the richer countries. Dr. Simon Yudkin, until recently a London paediatrician, reported only ninety-five deaths among four thousand admissions to his wards. Of these children only nineteen were more than one year old, and only eight experienced a long and frightening illness.[249]

My own experience is limited to the two or three children who died in the Hospices where I worked, so I shall have to draw heavily on the writings of others. Even then I have little to draw on since very few doctors have enough experience to write about the death of children. Surgeons who specialize in correcting congenital deformities, and physicians concerned with treating leukaemia, are the only people who see many children die, and they never get used to it.

Even people who are accustomed to dealing with children, therefore can be thrown off balance when a child is dying. Dr. Yudkin wrote :

"The dying child's questions and oblique references may not come to the parents or the consultant but to the registrar, house-man, schoolteacher, nurse, laboratory technician, or ward orderly. Should we all have reached a decision before the question is likely to be asked? Should we at least all have discussed it?"

In this branch of terminal care more than in any other, a prior discussion among all concerned is needed.

A Child's Approach to Death

Children grieve over the loss of someone close to them in the way that adults do.* They seldom give a thought to their own death, however, unless they are worried by a morbid fear. Before the age of about three they have no concept of death at all. Thereafter their understanding depends on the attitude of those around them. If it is pretended that Grandad never died but "went away" and when the subject is mentioned it is seen to embarrass the parents, then not only will a child pick up—for life—our modern taboo on death, but he may also imagine all kinds of terrifying things about it. These fantasies can be diverse and lurid. If they upset the child, he will need to be listened to carefully and gently, however much time it may take. This matter of time is vital because the child may only allude to his fears indirectly, and reassurance will have to be gentle and persistent. Doris Howell notes how much confidence can come from the use of well-tried liturgical prayers and services in the ward and sickroom.[96]

Maria Nagy asked nearly four hundred children in Budapest what they thought death was.[150] She found that their replies indicated three stages of understanding :

"The first is characteristic of children between three and five. They deny death as a regular and final process. Death is a departure, a further existence in changed circumstances. There are ideas too that death is temporary. Indeed distinction is made of degrees of death†.... Living and lifeless are not yet distinguished....

* See p. 133.
† A man may be "badly killed."

63

"In the second stage, in general between the ages of five and nine, death is personified, considered a person. Death exists but the children still try to keep it distant from themselves. Only those die whom the death-man carries off. Death is an eventuality. There also occur fantasies, though less frequently, where death and the dead are considered the same. In these cases they consistently employ the word death for the dead. Here death is still outside us and not universal. . . .

"Finally, in the third stage, in general around nine years, it is recognized that death is a process which takes place in us, the perceptible result of which is the dissolution of bodily life. By then they know that death is inevitable. At this age not only the conception as to death is realistic, but also their general view of the world."

It is interesting to reflect whether these three stages represent increasing or decreasing understanding.

Attending a morbid funeral may spark off fears of death in a child, but most of them will talk freely and easily about the subject. Alison Player made the following observations:

"A child may react variously and very strongly to the death of a member of his family, particularly the parent. Unconsciously he may feel the loss of his mother as a desertion, perhaps as a punishment for his own misbehaviour. . . . He may even feel that it is his own unconscious aggression to his parent which has killed him. . . . At the time of death very particularly, the child should have the opportunity to hear explanations of the truth given simply and calmly, his questions answered, and his feelings explicitly understood. The child is so vulnerable."[172]

Most children nowadays will never meet death, so it is usually a rather theoretical matter. When facing their own premature death, however, it is nearly always found that it looks less of a threat to the child than does the separation from his parents involved in moving into hospital. Distress over anticipating painful medical procedures, or over the death of another child in the ward, have been found far to outweigh the fear of death in most children.[151]

Dr. Walter Alvarez tells how a slightly older age group—the teenagers—may react with great disappointment and bitterness to being told a grave prognosis;[8] but as he and another great American physician, Dr. Alfred Worcester,* have pointed out, younger child-ren die very easily.

The Approach of the Caring Team

Though labelled "dying," they must remain as ordinary children, full of fun and wonder, not objects of pity or victims of cold scientific endeavour. Dr. Cicely Saunders says:

"I am sure I do not have to emphasize the importance of delight, of beauty and fantasy and of parties. This is the setting in which the patient can be allowed to talk, grumble or cry. This is the time when you talk about progress, about symptoms and their treatment, and allow questions. Fear is drained out of so many questions if they can be voiced."[197]

To enter a child's world and anticipate his fears and puncture the threat that seems to lodge in death, we have to be the very best people we know how to be. The following description of how the wise physician Sir William Osler behaved in the situation has been quoted by at least two other authors,[43, 104] but merits being repeated here:

"He visited our little Janet twice every day from the middle of October until her death a month later, and these visits she looked forward to with pathetic eagerness and joy.... Instantly the sickroom was turned into fairyland, and in fairy language he would talk about the flowers, the birds, and the dolls.... In the course of this he would manage to find out all he wanted to know about the little patient.

"The most exquisite moment came one cold, raw, November morning, when the end was near, and he brought out from his pocket a beautiful red rose, carefully wrapped in paper, and told how he had watched this last rose of summer growing in his garden and how the rose had called out to him as he passed by, that she wished to go along with him to see his 'little lassie.' That evening we had a fairy tea party, at a tiny table by the bed, Sir William talking to the rose, his little lassie and her mother in a most exquisite way ... and the little girl understood that neither fairies nor people could always have the colour of a red rose in their cheeks, or stay as long as they wanted to in one place, but that they nevertheless would be happy in another home and must

* See Bibliography.

not let the people they left behind, particularly their parents, feel badly about it; and the little girl understood and was not unhappy."

The secret is to give the child a sense of security, which means sharing with and trusting in someone else. "A child separated from its mother may be quite safe—but it feels very insecure. A child in its mother's arms during an air-raid may be very unsafe indeed— but it feels secure."[197]

If this trust is to grow, we must be strictly honest with children. They are much more alert than adults and detect lies easily.[48] Honesty means allowing the child to ask you, or tell you, anything he wishes. If bad news is to be given, this should be done with precision and tenderness. Idle or hasty reassurance cannot be precise, and is never tender. Neither, of course, is blurting out the "whole truth." If the child can trust those caring for him, and has the feeling that they are with him, on his side as it were, he will feel secure. If people try to avoid him or deceive him, he will feel vulnerable.

To be able to face death with a child, we must first be honest with ourselves. Are we trying to reassure ourselves when we lie to him, or when we go on plying him with uncomfortable treatments even after the battle is clearly lost? Dr. Yudkin pleads that we let the dying child die in peace. He says :

I am not, of course, referring to an acute crisis in illnesses which can perhaps be cured but, when the end is inevitable, although we feel the death of the child to be out of time, must we rush around with tubes, injections, masks, and respirators? Someone said recently that no one nowadays is allowed to die without being cured. Perhaps we do it only for the parents' sake; but perhaps we ourselves cannot accept our limitations. And can we sometimes consider whether the dying child should be allowed to die at home?"[249]

A lady whose son was born with major congenital abnormalities and lived for only one month, in a hospital, wrote to me as follows :

"I am devoted to the paediatrician who looked after him and to the Sister who was in charge, and yet I think they handled his life and death wrongly. I was not with him when he died. I expressed milk for him but after a while was not allowed to breast feed him as I wished to. Photographs were taken of him, tubes inserted, his head shaved, etc. He did not die in peace and I feel in retrospect that I should have lived his life with him and been with him when he died. It is complicated, I know, because there must be cases when babies' lives are saved by giving them apparently inhumane treatment. Also, though my paediatrician took me into the ward at first, he thought it better for my husband and two elder children if I went home to them. But I always remember my mother's account of her own mother nursing a dying baby (in 1884 or thereabouts), sitting all night by the fire with the baby in her arms, and him dying like that. She never forgot, because she told her daughter about it so vividly, years later; and it seemed to me that if one's children must die, that is the way for it to happen."

This does not preclude our being always on the lookout for signs of unexpected recovery. Amazing recoveries occur frequently enough with adults, but with children miracles are commonplace. A cautionary tale from my own experience illustrates this : One of the London teaching hospitals sent a boy of eight to die in St. Joseph's Hospice. He had a growing brain tumour and had lapsed into unconsciousness. The only signs of life were sighing, breathing and an occasional moan. In the next bed was a retired taxi driver who died a few weeks later, and he "adopted" the boy in a grandfatherly fashion. Passing the boy's bed one day, he remarked,

"I'm sure Hubert's asking for something."

"Not when he's unconscious!" said the sister.

"Yes he is," insisted Grandad, "listen." There followed a moan from Hubert.

"There you are!" came the triumphant exclamation, "He wants some orange juice."

Doubtfully Sister gave some in a feeding cup, and to everyone's surprise Hubert swallowed it, and distinctly asked for more. So we pulled out his feeding tube and fed him by mouth. Gradually consciousness returned, limbs moved which had hitherto been flaccid. Energetic physiotherapy was instituted. Soon Hubert was taking walks in the garden with the staff nurse and having speech therapy. Once he could run he became the life and soul of the ward : imagine having twenty-two indulgent Grandads! The tea boy and general giver of cheek started taking weekends at home, then went to a school for delicate children, and finally back to completely normal living. He is in excellent health to this day.

The Parents

The first hint that all is not well will come to the child from a change in his parents' behaviour. He will find that he can get away with more naughtiness than usual, and that they do not let him out of their sight. They start to grieve and cannot hide it.

Those caring for the family may have a very trying time. The parents often feel angry and want to blame someone bitterly : the family doctor did not diagnose what was wrong soon enough, the surgeon did not do the operation properly, the nurses did not make him comfortable enough, if Aunty Mary had not let them go swimming in the sea it would never have happened, if that car driver had kept to the speed limit . . . and so on. All this will have to be patiently listened to like weathering a storm.

Hill of Tarvit Marie Curie Home, Fife

Some families try to follow up every possibility of treatment. Certainly a visit to Lourdes, even if not followed by miracles, may be therapeutic for the whole family; but one should be wary of any expensive attempts at treatment which may cause distress to the young patient. There is no shortage of charlatans whose hocus pocus could be tried; some are sincere and some are positively mercenary.

The shorter the child's last illness, the sharper will be the reaction of the parents. Acceptance of the situation will be much easier for them if they have had time to grieve and adjust their outlook while he is still alive. This can be exasperating for the staff. Several times we had to calm the indignation of the nurses when one mother of a dying boy made complaints, or remade his bed, or hovered around interfering with nursing procedures. We had to impress on them the utter horror of the situation for her, and that she also was now our patient. In order that this grieving may be given time, and not come all in a flood, it is desirable that the parents are told of an inevitably fatal outcome at the earliest possible moment.

To relieve his parents' frustration at feeling so impotent before Michael's disease, we involved them as much as possible in his day to day care. Parents are very much part of the team. Not only should they be encouraged to help with the nursing, they may also want to be involved in the making of decisions. Some may prefer to leave all decisions to the doctor, particularly if they have a burden of guilty feelings to unload.[249] In one American hospital "Parents had regular educational conferences with the physicians in order to learn more about their children's diseases, the program of treatment, and the investigative program. The reception given by the parents was rewarding to the physicians."[151] Every family will want to partake in the supervision of their child to a different degree. There will be a different balance point for each. For some almost anything other than passive visiting will be too painful. Others will feel as if they are deserting their duty if they do not contribute to every decision. How we found this balance point with one particular couple may perhaps be instructive.

Ann was unconscious, following a crash in her boy friend's car, and her condition was deteriorating. When admitted for terminal care, she was found to have a chest infection. She did respond a little to stimulation, with a strange nasal cry. So one had to assume that some impressions were still being received, which meant that she just might still be suffering. Of course she would be given full nursing care, but the question arose as to whether she should be given antibiotics for the potentially fatal chest infection. From the patient's point of view, it would probably have been kinder to relieve distress and allow the pneumonia to kill her gently. But we feared that the parents would feel guilty at having consented to her admission to the Hospice if Ann died immediately. On the other hand they might be longing to see an end to her sufferings. So we decided to hold a case conference.

The parents, the doctors and the ward sister accordingly met over a cup of tea. We explained to them that the neurosurgeon had found irreparable damage, but that we could probably keep Ann alive for years if we dosed her with drugs. At first they urged that everything possible be done, until her father realized that this was for their sake only, and not for hers. "Will she always be like this?" he asked. This we confirmed and added that to preserve her life artificially *in this condition* for any length of time would feel wrong to us. The parents were certain that they wanted her present infection treated, just in case she showed any signs of recovery : they had not quite given up hope. Nevertheless, they also agreed that it would not be right to keep this going for years, and accepted that eventually we would have to stop treating her. "But if you do decide not to treat her," they said, "just do what you think best without telling us, so that we don't have to think about it." This perfect balance gave us a clear guide for the future and established firm trust between us all.

The end of the story is also salutary, because Ann showed some signs of improvement. Not only did she start to swallow again, but showed a distinct preference for being fed by her mother. Our hopes had risen so much that when she did develop another chest infection we had the dilemma all over again. In view of the improvement, we treated this infection as well. But this time the drugs failed to work; she had a series of fits and died. *L'homme propose, mais Dieu dispose.*

In his book *Death Comes Home*, the Rev. Simon Stephens lists four circumstances which can deepen the despair of the parents' grief : If the child were an only child, if surviving brothers or sisters showed disturbed behaviour due either to their own grief or to their receiving inadequate attention from distressed parents, if the death exacerbated some marital disharmony, or if the parents felt very guilty in connection with the child's death. As Mr. Stephens says : *

> "The element of guilt is a common factor in parental grief. The failure to see a child across a busy main road, to check the brakes on a recently renovated pedal cycle, or to change well-worn car tyres are just as likely to produce a guilt complex because of their disastrous consequences as is the suicide of a teenager. In such circumstances as these the element of guilt is always destructive and unless resolved in the company of a sympathetic friend may have grave repercussions."

* p. 84. See Bibliography.

The Society of Compassionate Friends* which the Rev. Stephens founded in Coventry now has branches all over Britain, enabling bereaved parents to meet and help one another. Its work has proved immensely valuable.

The tendency to idealize the dead is harmless provided that it does not encroach on our love for the living. "In cases where the dead child has been 'canonised' by his sorrowing parents to the exclusion of the other children," Mr. Stephens tells us, "it has been shown that the siblings become antisocial in a desperate bid to attract attention and to win back their parents' love." The mother may even have feelings of resentment towards her surviving children when they clamour for her notice, for she may feel that she owes it to the dead one to dwell morbidly on his loss.[172] Alternatively she may become over-protective, fearing that a similar fate may overtake his brothers and sisters, and deny them half the adventures of childhood.

Born Dying

When our baby daughter arrived and I took her from the midwife to hand to my wife, I just had to have a quick look for missing limbs, cleft lip, bifid spine and the like, in spite of myself. So much has been said recently about congenital deformities that many women have extreme anxiety until they have seen their new baby, and even so much as a contact with german measles sends them to their doctor in search of an abortion.

The vast majority of babies born with malformations live with them with only minor adjustments. But a few are incapable of independent existence, and soon die. In these cases the parents usually suffer a rather different kind of short, sharp grief.

Nowadays a few of these children pose a bizarre and torturing problem. Should they be resuscitated?[202] Should they be fed? Should their deformity be corrected by surgery in spite of probable mental deficiency? About 8% of all survivors of such operations are found to be severely handicapped and mentally affected. I am not in a position to decide on these questions: I can only repeat the arguments from opposing points of view.

Mr. Ellison Nash, a surgeon who operates on deformed neonates and then maintains a profoundly loving follow-up at Chailey Heritage, avers that a surgeon with this skill should examine all cases,

* Address on p. 130.

and operate whenever it is possible. He reasons that, when they are not operated on, these children do not all die, and it is not always possible to predict which ones will not. If they survive, their disabilities will be much worse than they would have been had operations been performed. For instance, children with hydrocephalus (a head swollen with fluid because the normal drainage channels are blocked) may go blind if an artificial valve is not inserted. They may then not die as expected.[58] He considers that the decision not to treat should only be taken when complications develop at the age of two or three in an infant who is showing signs of severe retardation.

Another surgeon, Mr. Lloyd-Roberts, wrote :

"We are confronted by a serious ethical problem in which the quantity of survival sometimes obscures the quality. The burden on the health and social services is immense.

"The tragedy is emphasized when we compare the infant, the child and the young adult with severe paralysis. The infant differs little from his normal fellow—both are wet and must be carried everywhere. Even the child of six has some appeal, gallantly coping with his handicap with calipers, crutches and urinary bag. At thirteen he has usually reverted to a wheelchair in which he sits, obsese, odiferous, acneiform and impotent, contemplating a sorry future with justifiable melancholy . . . neglect, which includes the withholding of antibiotics, will usually resolve the dilemma."[65, 124, 125]

Officials of the Association for Spina Bifida frowned on this pronouncement,[44, 45, 220] in particular the chairman for the Midlands who said,

"We should seriously consider the question of whether we are trying to produce a race of perfect human beings or taking the proper care of those we have. . . . As each supposedly hopeless case is treated, a little more is added to our knowledge of spina bifida, and to the chances of future generations of spina bifida children. . . . They should not be condemned because they pose a problem. . . ."[247]

Usually the parents will partake in the decision[32] whether or not to treat, as was pointed out in correspondence in *The Times*[220]

which followed the publication of Mr. Lloyd-Roberts' views. The dilemma of these parents was expressed by one mother as follows:

"Few parents of spina bifida children are able to adopt the clear-cut views of some of your correspondents. We are more likely to be living in a perpetual cloud of conflicting feelings.

"When my two-year-old son was born the team of doctors in charge thought his outlook was good and so operated immediately (they told me that if they did not operate he might not die but survive in a worse state). A year later we knew he would not only never walk but never even sit unsupported. Meanwhile he received from physiotherapists, doctors, social workers and all his family an immense amount of loving care. I think we all carry a double wish: that he will grow and prove intelligent and able to cope with life; and at the same time that he might die painlessly should life prove intolerable.

"The emotional pendulum swings one way when we read of families who cope or of children who seem happy; and when we realize how much support and encouragement our society offers. It swings the other way when we read of the horrors of life for institutionalized adolescents, and realize how many people would like the problem swept away drastically. One day I think I am a moral coward for not being prepared to solve it by drastic means myself; the next I reproach myself for insufficient courage and optimism in thinking of the future.

"There is certainly a good case for leaving spina bifida children unoperated at birth (though I wonder how many doctors would leave their own children); but I suspect that some of those who advance it are trying to tidy up the world in a way that can never be done. What about mongol children, spastics, children injured in accidents? In hospital waiting rooms I have been *envied* by other mothers for my bright strong-armed little boy...."

The whole controversy may be resolved in the next few years by improvement in the accuracy of prediction of a deformed child's chances of survival and health.

Open Questions

I can only echo Dr. Simon Yudkin in saying that in our care of dying children we still find more questions than answers. Because we are at a loss as to how relief can be brought to the child, we often concentrate on the parents instead—and certainly we have much help to offer them. But a genius to equal Osler and his wonderful approach is sadly wanting—we await wisdom. What will certainly not do is the coldly scientific attitude which thinks that pat answers to human problems can be found by analyses of data. Many papers reveal this shallow approach, using such sick expressions as "a human love object" and "family homeostasis" as a substitute for accurate observation. When we approach dying children we must do so with deep humility and open hearts, however much it hurts.

St. Christopher's Hospice, Sydenham

7

The Right Time to Die

So when at last the Angel of the darker drink
Of Darkness finds you by the river-brink,
And, proferring his Cup, invites your Soul
Forth to your Lips to quaff it—do not shrink.
Rubaiyat of Omar Khayyam

THE duty of a doctor is to restore his patients to health. For some he cannot do this, but he can keep them at least in reasonable shape, jogging along as useful individuals. But for some others he can do neither: for these the *healthy* thing to do is to die.

It is proposed that there is a right time to die; that this time may come before a man has breathed the very last breath of which his body is capable; and that an experienced physician can recognize, or learn to recognize, that this right time to die has come. Please understand that what is proposed is to refrain from prolonging life beyond the right time, NOT to hasten the termination of life in any way. I will deal with euthanasia in the next chapter. What worries people, particularly nurses, is the prospect of the senile and suffering being kept alive, and not the question of euthanasia at all: that is just a red herring.[117, 165, 215]

75

Care of the Dying

This is a problem without precedent, since we have acquired the ability significantly to delay death only in this century. There are no traditional ethics in medicine, in the church, or in the law, to guide us in problems related to resuscitation and terminal care.

Watching a patient and responding appropriately to his real needs is so much more intelligent and precise than a blunderbuss type of medicine which mechanically applies a standard treatment for each diagnosis, irrespective of the patient's age, health or maturity. Lord Amulree coined the term "medicated survival," and made a plea for medical students to be taught what are the limits of treatment.[9, 198] They must be shown that a man's death does not represent a humiliating defeat of medicine, but is the logical conclusion to life. To die well is a great achievement, a very positive step which makes a man so much the greater, so much more completely a man. Good terminal care will enable him to take this step —that is what it is all about.[196]

Elderly people will often make the point that they are quite ready to die, and find the prospect not in the least alarming.[171, 217] A change of mind which is not resignation, but preparation, becomes evident as death approaches. Active treatment and attempts at vigorous mobilization would now be out of place. Just because we can do something at this stage, it does not follow that it is either right or kind always to do it.[195] When a patient is seen to be preparing for death, this is something we should respect. It is not at all the same thing as the wilful decision of the suicide, or the arrogant demand of the euthanasiast, but a real change in the man's outlook and understanding. A trust, a relaxation, a contentment, a willing giving up, are all evident.[233] If a patient who is dying does not take this step, which is the last big step of life, then one should seriously consider whether one's care was deficient. It is a legitimate medical decision to abandon *cure*, but never to abandon *care*.

I remember how, when my grandmother realized that she had a breast cancer (in 1960, before the present high rate of cure for this condition) she drew out her savings from the bank and went on an expensive shopping spree. My mother was puzzled, but accompanied her as she bought shoes, silk stockings, lacy underwear, a smart costume, matching hat and handbag and a pair of white gloves. They were all carefully stored in drawers and cupboards (with mothballs, I'm afraid!), and the mystery deepened. Then, on the day of her death, she asked to be fully decked out in the whole outfit "because I'm going before God today." She was too busy with these preparations to be worried about the actual process of dying.

A Mrs. P. whom I knew, had evaded difficulties throughout her life. With much help from the Hospice team, however, she faced them all in her last three months of life. There was a problem with her two daughters: the elder had been her favourite, so that her relations with the younger one were cold and strained. With psychiatric help she was able to open up to the girl for the first time, and be friends. Mrs. P. cross-examined me about her cancer several times, always indicating what reply she wanted. But the last time, she put up no defences at all, and just asked "Am I dying?" She insisted that I should be honest, and she showed great interest, but was in no way upset. Later that week she saw the Chaplain, at my suggestion, because she had made some comment about Judgement which I thought was more in his province. Having thus come slowly to terms with the family, her disease, and finally with God, she died at the right time of pneumonia, which we did not try to cure.

The Old Man's Friend

Yet not his ghost; O let him pass! he hates him
That would upon the rack of this tough world
Stretch him out longer.

—*King Lear*, Act 5, Sc. 3

When not to treat is usually self-evident.[1, 169] Apart from anything else, doctors are not as powerful as the layman often thinks. The decision to treat an elderly person's pneumonia is no guarantee of cure. It becomes obvious to any geriatrician that while some patients are treatable, others have lived their allotted span, and cannot be resurrected by any treatment. Geriatric decisions need to be based on common sense and compassion, rather than on a spirit of adventure.

Sir William Osler called bronchopneumonia "The Old Man's Friend" because it is the usual ultimate cause of death for someone already weakened by a chronic disease. It usually induces a quiet, peaceful death—quite unlike pneumonia in a younger person. The fear that we may banish this friend from the bedside is not well founded, since treatment often fails, but it is our efforts to banish him which can give patients great discomfort. Treatment with antibiotics is much more likely to be successful when the younger sufferer from advanced cancer contracts pneumonia. The results can be catastrophic, if doctors have their priorities wrong and tacitly accept longevity as the aim, at any price.[30, 69, 109] We certainly need good techniques, but as Sir Theodore Fox pointed out,[95] we also need to know when to use them.

In a case like this the first decision that has to be made is whether the illness is terminal. If it is regarded as such, the whole caring team then becomes involved in a combined effort to bring comfort to the patient as he dies. Decisions should now be taken collectively : the nurses, chaplain, physiotherapist and relatives should all be consulted. There can be no absolute rules with so fine a creature as a Man, and in some cases the decision will be the patient's own. For some people death will be a quick release, for others the dignified way to die will be in fighting to the last.

A doctor may have to be gently firm over his decision to refrain from meddlesome therapy, because nurses or relatives may press him to *do* something if, for instance, a dying patient's breathing becomes laboured.[2, 69] This may be uncomfortable to watch, but the patient is usually unconscious in the final stages of terminal pneumonia,[18] and any treatment given at this stage would be therapy for the watchers rather than for the patient. To secure a peaceful end for the patient, the doctor or ward sister may have to point out that interference at this point would be what Sir George Pickering called "false charity." One doctor even dubbed penicillin —the mainstay of treatment for pneumonia—"the old man's enemy !"[11, 168]

When to Resuscitate

Is life a boon? If so it must befall
That death, whene'er he call,
Must call to soon.

Is life a thorn? Then count it not a whit!
Then count it not a whit—
Man is well done with it.

W. S. Gilbert in
The Yeoman of the Guard.

Dying is normal—a healthy thing to do; everyone does it! Death is not an enemy to be swatted and parried to the last grim moment.

When I was a junior physician in a hospital, we were once called urgently to the bedside of a lady of ninety. The nurse used the term "cardiac arrest"—the old lady's heart had stopped (as hearts are apt to do, around ninety!). But because the cardiac arrest alarm was raised, I and the other houseman launched into a full-scale resuscitation. With violent drugs injected direct into the heart, blasts of electric current through her chest, noise and chaos, she had anything but a peaceful death. On reflection we realized that all this had been inappropriate,[103] but nothing in our medical student training gave us any guide. Indeed once the feeling of emergency is in the air, there is not time to weigh up the pros and cons. The decision is rarely a doctor's anyway, because usually the only person on the scene when an emergency occurs is a nurse— probably a relatively junior one if it is night-time—and she decides whether or not to resuscitate. Needless to say, it is a courageous nurse who decides not to. Once things have started, it is very difficult for the doctor when he arrives to stop everything, particularly if the patient is showing signs of reviving.

Clearly, what is required is a prior discussion, involving the whole team, to consider just to what *kind* of life they would be restoring the patient. They must ask themselves "Are we hoping to return the patient to health, or are we to regard him as a terminal case who, if he dies, is to be left in peace and not resurrected?"[156, 166] For the patient with a less dramatic form of fatal illness—say a spreading cancer or a creeping paralysis like motor neurone disease, a similar question needs to be answered : "What is our aim with this particular patient?"

If no definite answer presents itself, then one will institute what Professor Duncan Vere called a "trial of therapy."[228] Treatment of the patient's condition is started, and he is watched closely to see if it helps. If no progress is made, then the treatment is discontinued at once. The parallel is in midwifery, where the obstetrician watching beside someone who, he anticipates, may have difficulty in childbirth, allows a "trial of labour." At the first sign of anything going wrong he abandons the trial for a Caesarian operation.

It is easy to hope for omnipotence from doctors, but when all is said and done it is good nursing which keeps people alive more than any medical pyrotechnics.[1] Many a pneumonia is fatal in

MED A 521153
5

NOTICE TO INFORMANT

I hereby give notice that I have this day signed
a medical certificate of the cause of death
of .....Mrs. Mary xxxxxxx

Signature R. Amorton.

Date..... 2.4.70

This notice must be given by the Certifying Medical
Practitioner to the person who is qualified and liable
to act as informant for the purpose of the registration
of the death. As to the person liable to act as
informant, see back.

DUTIES OF INFORMANT

This notice is to be delivered by the informant to the
registrar of births and deaths for the sub-district in
which the death occurred. The death cannot be registered until the medical certificate has reached the
registrar. Failure to deliver this notice to the registrar
renders the informant liable to prosecution.

*The informant must be prepared to state accurately
to the registrar the following particulars:—*

(1) The date and place of death, and the deceased's
usual address, (2) the full names and surname, (and
the maiden surname if the deceased was a woman who
had married), (3) the date and place of birth (town
and county; or country if born abroad), (4) the
occupation (and the name and occupation of her
husband if the deceased was a married woman or a
widow), (5) whether deceased was in receipt of a
pension, or allowance from public funds and (6) if
deceased was married, the age of the surviving widow
or widower.

DECEASED'S MEDICAL CARD MUST
BE DELIVERED TO THE REGISTRAR

MED A 521153
5

Registrar to enter
No. of Death Entry
....

BIRTHS AND DEATHS REGISTRATION ACT 1953
(Form prescribed by the Registration of Births Deaths, and Marriages Regulations 1968)

MEDICAL CERTIFICATE OF CAUSE OF DEATH

For use only by a Registered Medical Practitioner WHO HAS BEEN IN ATTENDANCE during the deceased's last illness, and
to be delivered by him forthwith to the Registrar of Births and Deaths

Name of deceased Mrs. Mary xxxxxxx

Date of death as stated to me 2nd day of April 19 70 Age as stated to me 84

Place of death Raphael Ward, St. Joseph's Hospice, London E.8.

Last seen alive by me 1st day of April 19 70

* 1 The certified cause of death takes account of
2 Information obtained from post-mortem.
3 Information from post-mortem may be available later.*
  Post-mortem not being held.

    a Seen after death by me.
    b Seen after death by another medical practitioner
    but not by me.
    c Not seen after death by a
    medical practitioner.

CAUSE OF DEATH

These particulars not to be
entered in death register

Approximate interval
between onset and death

I

Disease or condition directly leading
to death ... ...

(a) She died of old age.

due to (or as a consequence of)

(b) ....
due to (or as a consequence of)

(c) ....

Antecedent causes,
Morbid conditions, if any, giving
rise to the above cause stating the
underlying condition last.

II

Other significant conditions, contributing to the death, but not related
to the disease or condition causing it.

II ....

....

I hereby certify that I was in medical attendance during the above named deceased's last illness, and that the
particulars and cause of death above written are true to the best of my knowledge and belief.

Signature R. Amorton.

Qualifications as
registered by
Medical Council } M.R.C.S. L.R.C.P.

Residence St. Joseph's Hospice. E.8. Date 2.4.70

Please ring appropriate digit and letter.
† This does not mean the mode of dying, such as heart failure, asphyxia, asthenia, etc.; it means the disease, injury, or complication which caused death.

SEE BACK

spite of antibiotics, and many resolve in spite of not being treated. Even the most bizarre and violent treatments give very limited returns in terms of lengthened life. One American paper tells a series of stories of patients with terminal illnesses who were rehabilitated (aged 92, with a fractured hip, pneumonia and senile dementia), force fed (aged 86, with a collapsed spine and too weak to fight off the feeding nurses), and resuscitated (aged 80, with a stroke which left him mute and paralysed, followed by a second one which rendered him comatose). Here are two passages from the third of these case histories :

"The attending physician was ensnared in the family's death wishes and provided a vacuum of medical and nursing guidance. Indeed, he expressed his desire to the nursing staff that nothing be done for the patient : 'The patient is terminal and should be permitted to die peacefully.'

"The nursing staff, however, had become attached to the patient during his stay at the institution. They insisted they be permitted to feed the patient and engage in a total nursing care program, including restorative care.

"The director of nursing received permission from the medical director of the institution to address her wishes to the attending physician on the basis that *the nursing staff had a clear commitment to maintain life* (my italics) and was under no obligation to be the agent of the death wishes of family or physician. The attending physician relented and permitted the nursing staff to feed the patient via nasogastric tube, thus providing an adequate intake of fluid and electrolytes, calories, vitamins and medication. A restorative nursing program, including physical therapy, was instituted. . . . The patient was once again able to be transferred from bed to chair and to ambulate with assistance in the parallel bars. He expired five months later from an additional massive stroke."[139]

This idea that doctors and nurses must preserve life at all costs is an odd one, and quite new. Never has this been their duty. The famous Hippocratic Oath required a doctor to swear by the God of Health, but not by Life. His concern should always be with the good health of the whole man, not with the longevity of his body.

The principle to guide us in decisions about life and death was (and I write as a non-Catholic) beautifully delineated by Pope Pius XII,[170] who distinguished between ordinary and extraordinary measures. Ordinary treatment means whatever a patient can obtain and undergo without thereby imposing an excessive burden on himself or others.[21]

It is only experience which can teach a doctor how to discriminate in this kind of situation. Not long ago we thought that a flat electro-encephalogram (i.e. the absence of any electrical activity in the brain) indicated that a man was dead. Now every intensive care unit has stories of people who were comatose with a flat E.E.G., and apparently dead for weeks or even months, and then began to recover. The question of when to turn off the drips and respirators whereby the patient with brain damage is artificially given food and breath, has thus been hit back into the doctor's court. No rules are available. He can only say that if there is no brain activity for many weeks, and the patient's condition looks as if it is deteriorating, the time has come to turn off.[223] It is obvious that the machines have to be stopped at some point, otherwise beds would be used for years in maintaining corpses while waiting lists of the living grew longer.[113, 239] Here again the decision is not as difficult as is widely supposed. One anaesthetist said to me, "It's simple really : I just go into the ward and look at him. If he's dead I turn it off, and if he's still there I don't." In an age of measurement and science we are fearful of clinical judgement and have come to mistrust the evidence of our own senses. Events are forcing us, however, to face up to situations in which we have no other guide.

As an editorial in the *Lancet* said,

"It is part of the clinician's duty to recognize the inevitability of death in certain situations and to avoid the unnecessary physical and emotional trauma associated with unsuccessful attempts at resuscitation. . . ."[116]

The same applies to surgeons, who have been admonished not to operate on the elderly without very good cause. Sir David Smithers said,

"It is no great tribute to the art of surgery to see a feeble old gentleman dragging out his life for a few months cured of an advanced pharyngeal carcinoma* if deprived of many things which might have made these few months tolerable."

His words were echoed by Sir Stanford Cade, another distinguished surgeon.[31, 36, 206] There is even a limit to what nurses should attempt. Forcibly to feed the dying robs them of dignity,[216] and nurses are sometimes very worried by the forcible administration of drugs. Indeed, this has already led to the scandalous dismissal of one hospital sister who declined to give an antibiotic to an aged patient who refused it. The doctor argued that as the patient was confused, other people should decide what was good for her. But the sister said that the lady's decision was a very reasonable one. "Why are you making me have these medicines, you cruel one?" she asked. Under the circumstances it was incumbent upon the doctor to inject the drugs forcibly himself—nurses should certainly never be obliged to do anything against their conscience. In a book produced by the Medical Protection society,† J. Leahy Taylor even went as far as to say "It can hardly be thought proper to deprive a patient of right to decline consent solely because he happens to be detained under the Mental Health Act."

The Legal Position

Anyone who is worried that treatment to themselves or a relative may constitute "meddlesome medicine," should discuss this with their own doctor. It may also help to contact the Patients' Association, which may be able to investigate the case.

In 1961 a case was considered in Sweden, where a Dr. Sallin stopped the intravenous drip treatment of a lady in her eighties who had an irreversible cerebral haemorrhage. Not until February 1965 was he finally acquitted of charges of killing.

No real test cases have yet come before British Courts, but of course we are free to refuse any medical treatment at any time. It is supposed that if a doctor was sued for assault by a patient whom he had revived when that patient had refused treatment and hoped to die, the court might uphold the doctor. He would, however, have to show that there was an element of confusion in the patient's other behaviour at the time. If the patient was resuscitated against his will without being consulted, he would probably be awarded "½p damages." In America, however, it has been upheld several times that a doctor in these circumstances is guilty of assault.

In English Common Law, all surgery or administration of potent

---

* Cancer of the upper throat.
† The Doctor and the Law, 1970, p. 99.

drugs technically constitutes an assault whether the patient consents or not, so that any kind of medicine can only be justified by appeal to the "Doctrine of Necessity." This requires that the evil averted be greater than the evil performed. Obviously this applies to all routine surgery. Also it is asserted that only as much evil may be done as is reasonably necessary to avert the greater evil. Thus a surgeon had to defend himself energetically in court when, in the course of removing a gall bladder, he incidentally removed the patient's appendix as well. (He was acquitted, but only because he could present statistics to show that an inflamed gall bladder frequently disturbs the health of the appendix as well.)

The withdrawal of useless treatment to avoid prolonging the process of dying could be justified by the doctrine of necessity,[144] and so could the giving of treatment which, in relieving the suffering of the dying, would possibly hasten their demise. Euthanasia could not be so justified, as we shall see in the next chapter.

One is almost tempted to hope for a "Bill for the Protection of the Rights of Old People" to enable the aged to refuse heroic treatments more effectively.[82] This story, entitled "Fools Rush In" appeared in the Christmas edition of the *Guy's Gazette* in 1969:

"Pertinax," said Aunt Agatha, "Are you now a Real Doctor?"
"Yes, aunt," replied Pertinax, "If this evening the cry went up, 'Is there a doctor in the house?' it would be my duty to respond. Aunt Agatha muttered something that sounded like "Fools rush in," and applied herself to her programme.

Pertinax glanced idly round the concert hall; it was definitely not his idea of a celebration to see Sir Bultitude Baton conducting on his hundredth birthday, but Aunt A. was not a bad old trout and had sound views on food and drink; her choice of seats was less satisfactory, from the upper box it was impossible to see the face of the girl with the gorgeous hair in the second violins. However, he had had a good dinner, was pleasantly drowsy, and could contemplate his future glorious career in peace. (... "Sir Pertinax Perforans was mercifully present on this occasion, and at the famous performer's side in a moment" ...). Sir Bultitude took his place amidst the plaudits of the audience; cellos led the orchestra into the dreamy strains of the first movement, Pertinax following them into the rosy glow of the future.

Suddenly, there was a crash and Pertinax started up to see that the tympani had, on this occasion, been augmented by the contact of Sir Bultitude's spare form with the platform. It was a matter of seconds only for Pertinax to leap from the box and, snatching a trumpet from its astonished owner, to sink on his knees by the side of the unconscious centenarian. Heart sounds came there none. Beckoning to the First Horn, as having a good respiratory excursion, he demonstrated in less than four seconds the most efficient method of administering the Kiss of Life, and started to open Sir Bultitude's shirt. This was, unfortunately, impossible to do at short notice, as the wearer was of the old school, and the front was inseparable from the studs owing to its resemblance to sheet-iron. There was not a moment to be lost, so Pertinax merely tore off the tie and wing collar, and applied himself to cardiac massage through the glacial expanse, occasionally reminding the First Horn that it was unnecessary to turn this particular recipient of his breath over from time to time to "empty him out."

Minutes passed, the First Horn had been replaced by the Second, then by the Trumpets, followed by the Woodwinds, and Pertinax began to realize that even he might soon have to call upon the Kettledrum to relieve him for a short space. The rest of the orchestra sat mute, the audience silent and amazed, reporters were writing shorthand at a tremendous speed, and even a quiet little man who had come on the platform murmuring "Sir Bultitude's personal geriatrician," was stunned into inaction by the brilliance of Pertinax's technique.

After what seemed like hours, Sir Bultitude stirred, his right hand straying feebly towards his chest. Signing to the Piccolo to desist, Pertinax bent down to catch the barely audible syllables from the trembling lips, "Angels ... fear ..." Of course, thought Pertinax, the old man could not realise his deliverance, and was fumbling for some religious medal. Tenderly, the younger man slipped his hand beneath the now battered shirt-front and drew out a small disc, a gesture which brought forth tumultuous applause from the over-tensed audience and orchestra, and as he did so, his eyes fell upon the words, "Please do *not*, repeat NOT attempt resuscitation." As the eyes of Sir Bultitude opened and fixed him with a venomous stare Pertinax closed his own.

The thunderous applause continued, and Pertinax felt a sharp poke in his ribs : "Wake up," said Aunt Agatha's voice. Pertinax opened his eyes and looked down on the platform where Sir

Bultitude was shaking hands with the Leading Violin. "I think we will go down to the bar," said Aunt Agatha; Pertinax agreed.

It was Thomas Jefferson, at the age of seventy-three, who wrote to a friend "I enjoy good health: I am happy in what is around me, yet I assure you I am ripe for leaving all, this year, this day, this hour." This readiness for death is common in the elderly. I recall waking up old Mrs. McP. after her first night in the Hospice. She peeped over the bedclothes at me with wondering eyes, looking at my white coat, the white sheets and the white uniforms of the nursing nuns. With breathless delight she asked me, "Am I in 'eaven?"

The Last Enemy

The last words of the great surgeon William Hunter, whispered to a friend as he lay dying, were "If I had strength to hold a pen I should write how easy and pleasant a thing it is to die."

It is our modern evasion of the subject and utter refusal even to believe in it that is at the root of some of our crazy attempts to resurrect the very aged. All kinds of errors follow as we attempt to conceal death from ourselves, from society and from the dying themselves. Sedation with drugs at the approach of death, for instance, if instituted for the sole purpose of preventing the dying person from dying consciously, is a regrettable practice, particularly for religious patients.[66]

One particular denial which amused me arose when an old lady died after a long period in a geriatric home. She had no particular fatal illness, but had just faded out normally and peacefully, so on the death certificate I wrote "She died of old age." It is reproduced in this book (Figure B) because I still have it: The Registrar returned it to me, objecting that I had not written down an acceptable diagnosis. If I did not change it, the Coroner would carry out an autopsy examination and *find* a diagnosis. So I let the official concerned dictate a proposed diagnosis to me, and I put it in inverted commas. I would have liked to pursue this comic turn to its illogical conclusion, but a post mortem examination would have distressed the family. The incident underlines, however, to what extent our present day society fears death: In the modern view it is pathological, not normal: it is horrible, not welcome: it is not allowed on the National Health!

The Captives (By "E.R.T.", in the *Nursing Mirror*, 17.12.71)

"Our scene is over; let us go home now."
"No, no", said they, "for us it's not half done;
We do not want the end, so why should you?"
"Because," we said, "we're ready to be gone."

"Into the dark?" they cried, "no, stay with us;
Into that fearful dark you shall not go.
Once you go there, you never will return;
Last time you started out, we drew you back."

St. Joseph's Hospice, Hackne

8

The Euthanasia Debate

SINCE I cannot put the case for euthanasia with much conviction, I would refer the reader to the bibliography at the back of this book for works which put the case cogently and forcefully.

As I understand it the humanist wants to control life and death. He wants to be kept alive until he decides to go, and then have euthanasia administered. This idea is based on a truth, hence its power. Men do have the freedom to make and execute this decision, because at their full stature, men are gods (Psalm 82:6 and John 10:30–38 confirm this for any Christian among my readers who may need such confirmation). It is, however, rare for a man to stand at his full stature, particularly when smitten by pain and disease. Some would choose to live too long—and as I pointed out in the previous chapter, there is a right time to die. Others would decide to die as a variation on running away. Now they emigrate to New Zealand; euthanasia, like suicide, would give them an even more distant haven.

Man is so much more natural than the humanist supposes. He does not have to conquer Nature, only to obey her, for his maximum happiness and freedom. We do not fly aeroplanes, for example, by conquering the air, but by obeying its laws of aero-dynamics.

Definitions

The word "euthanasia" comes from the Greek for a good death. Nowadays it does not mean that, but has a more precise conno-tation.[91] It involves one person killing another, either to relieve him of suffering which could not be relieved by any other means, or because he does not appear to be capable of sanity. Let us consider what euthanasia is and what it is not:[227]

1. In the days before morphine and similar opiate pain-killers were used properly, such large doses sometimes had to be given to relieve pain that the breathing was also suppressed. This side effect often shortened the patient's life. The Pope[170] and other moralists, the law, and medical ethics all considered this practice to be both moral and praiseworthy. This hastening of death was never an example of euthanasia, because the treatment was not designed to kill. If death did result, it was an unavoidable side effect. The situation is now of theoretical interest only, since it is medically inexcusable to use pain-killers so clumsily. As explained on pages 46-47, modern methods of pain control do not shorten life, and seldom even impair consciousness. It has often been suggested that doctors deliberately overdosed the patient with morphine, and that legalizing euthanasia would only be acknowledging what is already going on. But a doctor who wanted to kill someone could do it much more effectively and less obviously than that. Morphine would be a hopelessly blunt instrument for the job, and would have to be given in really enormous doses. This is not common medical practice, and never has been.

2. The withdrawing of artificial means of prolonging life was dealt with in the last chapter. This is not euthanasia, it is just good medicine. It is already legal and no change in the law is required. It is merely acting upon a recognition that a test—a trial of therapy—has yielded a negative result.

3. To refrain from giving inappropriate treatment is not euthanasia either. For instance, if a man has lost a large slice of brain in a road accident, but still goes on breathing, he should not be given antibiotics to prevent infection of the wound! It is a legitimate

medical judgement to decide that it is not in the interest of the patient to resuscitate him.

4. Suicide is another form of killing. This has not been a crime in Britain since 1961, because we cannot lay upon a man the duty always to be rational and never to be depressed. The duty (a moral, not a legal duty) lies with others to prevent him reaching a suicidal state. But if other people are not around when he does try to kill himself, so runs the reasoning, it would be cruel to brand him a criminal.

5. What *is* illegal is assisted suicide,[210] in every country except Uruguay (and special exceptions are made in France, Scotland, some of the United States and Switzerland). If one person urges or helps another to kill himself, this is a crime. The logic of the law's position is simple : A man strong enough to kill himself is strong enough to meet and survive adversity provided he is given enough help. If I find a man about to commit suicide, it is my duty to urge him not to do it, to care for him in such a way that he does not want to do it, and to put him in touch with social agencies that will ensure that he does not need to do it. If I just agree and help him, it is because I am too lazy to care and to fulfil my duty towards him. And afterwards, who could be sure I had not murdered him? cf. 244

6. Voluntary euthanasia is homicide by request, the person doing the killing being a doctor or nurse, and the person doing the requesting being the patient himself. The legalization of this measure was proposed in the House of Lords in 1936 by Lord Ponsonby,[85] using a bill largely drawn up by the President of the Society of Medical Officers of Health, Dr. C. Killick Millard.[138] This gentleman founded the Euthanasia Society which in 1969 changed its name to the Voluntary Euthanasia Society. The matter was discussed again in the Lords in 1950, when Lord Chorley moved for Papers,[86] but it was not until 1969 that another Bill was put before the House, this time by Lord Raglan.[87, 230] Finally in 1970 Dr. Hugh Gray asked permission to bring in a Private Member's Bill to the House of Commons, but leave was not granted.[88]

All these attempts to alter the Law of England were concerned only with voluntary euthanasia. This would be administered to those suffering severely from incurable disease. The patient concerned would have to sign a form requesting euthanasia. If he still wanted it one month later, a doctor could kill him, and if he ratified his decision three years later, the declaration would remain in force for the rest of his life unless he revoked it.

7. Involuntary euthanasia has also been suggested.[153] Professor Glanville Williams defended the idea of its use for "hopelessly defective infants" (*Euthanasia and the Right to Death*, Ed. A. B. Downing, p. 145). Lord Ailwyn, speaking in support of Lord Raglan's Bill, said it mercifully lit a torch *in the right direction* (my italics). He had just visited a low standard geriatric ward, and described it with horror. "Here it was," he said, "in all its pathetic reality, the crying need to offer these poor creatures the one remedy one felt in one's bones that they might accept gratefully and thankfully grasp." He said it was a melancholy thought to "withhold from them this boon, this milk of human kindness"—"to be wafted painlessly into the life to come." Quoting the words of St. Paul, Lord Ailwyn suggested that euthanasia would be the ultimate charity : "And now abideth faith, hope, charity, these three; but the greatest of these is charity." Charity of this mighty order would effectively knock out the faith and hope! Lord Ailwyn's final solution would be such a saving to the nation, because we would never have to bother with good geriatric care (the other solution[27, 99, 100]).

Lord Chorley also, when initiating the debate in 1950, said, "Another objection is that the Bill* does not go far enough, because it applies to adults and does not apply to children who come into the world blind, deaf and crippled, and who have a much better case than those for whom the Bill provides. That may be so, *but we must go step by step.*" (my italics)

The argument that legalization of voluntary euthanasia would be the thin end of a wedge is unquestionably valid : that is the expressed intention of its proponents. Suggestions such as these prompt many people, notably Roman Catholics, to say that voluntary euthanasia would just be softening the public resistance to much more dangerous legislation.[90] Clearly their fears are not groundless, particularly when you consider the escalation of abortion following the 1967 Act.[219]

8. To complete the list I will mention that killing someone in self defence or in war has always been accepted as legal, and death due to carelessness ranks as manslaughter, not murder.

* i.e. the 1936 one.

9. Finally, murder and genocide are universally accepted as wrong. It is interesting to reflect that it is not easy to say just why they are wrong—the best reason being simply because we all feel it is wrong. This natural inhibition is the basis of civilization, and deeply to be respected. One fears any inroad upon it, particularly during a period of moral decline.

The fact that the only government which allowed euthanasia was also one which indulged in both murder and genocide adds further fire to the opposition to euthanasia. This is regrettable because emotional outbursts about Nazis do not help rational debate.

The Case for Voluntary Euthanasia

A man should have the right to decide how much suffering he is prepared to accept.[204] When that limit is reached, it should be a basic human right for a man to lay down his life.[57] He may have used it well, finished all he started, be content to go, and have a terminal disease. Then follows what Lord Dawson described in the House of Lords, in 1936 as a "gap." During this time life is useless to the man. His weakness increases gradually attended by mounting suffering. He sees his family anxious and exhausted by nursing him. As Lord Dawson said,

"... the shortening of the gap should not be denied when the need is there. This is due not to a diminution of courage, but rather to a truer conception of what life means and what the end of its usefulness deserves."

The sum of human suffering would be reduced by the introduction of voluntary euthanasia, so it must be a good measure, and this is why Plato and St. Thomas More both advocated it.[77, 224] And did not Jesus say, "Greater love hath no man than this, that a man lay down his life for his friends" (John 15 : 13; John 10 : 18)?[234]

The fact that Christian ethics are traditionally opposed to euthanasia and suicide is irrelevant, since most of our modern society is not Christian. The minority who are, have no right to impose their opinions on the whole nation. Anyway, Christians are divided on the matter. Dean Inge of St. Paul's said "I do not think we can assume that God wills the prolongation of torture for the benefit of the soul of the sufferer."[231]

Doctors would soon come round to the idea when they realized that it lifted from their shoulders an agonizing decision.[214, 232] They could apply all their techniques of resuscitation until such time as the patient indicated that he had had enough : no longer need they worry about when to stop their treatments, or about people dying in great discomfort due to over-zealous treatment.[203] Further, when someone developed humiliating senile dementia, if he had signed the form previously, his family and the State could be relieved of the onerous job of looking after him.[56]

It cannot be stressed enough that the proposal is only for *voluntary* euthanasia. A patient who wanted his life prolonged would be free to have it prolonged, and need not sign the form. No-one would be brow-beaten into signing. No-one would be killed who had not asked to be. No doctor or nurse who objected on grounds of conscience would be obliged to co-operate in the killing.

That, as well as I can put it, is the case *for* euthanasia, and while it is nonsense in my opinion, it is only fair to include these views.

Legal Considerations

I shall first consider the principles on which basic human rights depend, and then look at euthanasia in the context of these rights.

When Moses summarized his law, he gave ten commandments and did not mention rights at all. The English Common Law works in the same way, and yet we in this country rejoice in greater freedom than almost any other. Here is how Maitland explained the working of law in his *Constitutional History of England* :*

> "Now the great mass of our ordinary criminal law is made up of prohibitions, of the imposition of negative duties, its language is 'Thou shalt do no murder', 'Thou shalt not steal' and so forth. It does not say 'Thou shalt succour thy neighbour in distress'— I commit no crime by not pulling my neighbour out of the water, though thereby I could save his life without wetting my feet. So again our law as to civil injuries, 'Torts' as we call them, consists of prohibitions—I am not to assault or slander or defraud my neighbour, trespass on his land or damage his goods. Generally it takes some contract or some special relationship or some office to create an active duty. In the greater number of cases in which anyone is bound actively to do something, he is bound because he has agreed to be bound."

* Cambridge University Press, 1968, p. 501.

The secret which makes Magna Carta and Moses' Pentateuch great codes of law allowing considerable freedom to the men governed under them is their clear and precise statement of the duties of a citizen. I have rights because other men observe their duties, not the other way about. I have the right to walk the streets of England without let or hindrance only so long as no-one attacks or robs me. If they do, of what value to me is my right? I have the right to a secure home until someone pillages it. If a burglar or an official of customs and excise breaks in, where has my right gone? Rights follow from the observations of duties by the community. Therefore good laws tell a man his duties. Weak law speaks of his rights, and is almost unenforceable, because there has to be a court argument to prove that the injuring party is acting unconstitutionally. This involves weeks of legal wrangling, whereas it is easy to prove that someone has failed in a specific duty.

Any "right to death" involves a corresponding duty to kill. To say there are conscience clauses in the Bill is no help.[143] As with abortion, the public would soon, quite correctly, be demanding euthanasia as a right, and putting pressure on dissenting doctors.

"Thou shalt do no murder" permits of no legal disputes, no governmental misapplication. It is a natural law. It states my duty. If the State exacts this duty from all, then I am safe; free to come and go, free from fear. My liberty is not curtailed by having to observe this duty towards others.

From what do such duties spring? Clearly they are universal. They are owed by the Prime Minister, the foreign visitor, the policeman, the Bishop, the Lord Mayor and me. They are owed to everyone, and any exceptions have to be specially defined by specific laws (such as the Mental Health Act which permits a doctor to detain an insane man for his own and other people's safety). If the duties of a citizen are not observed, the result is a loss of freedom by the whole community. If I cannot make an aeroplane journey without danger of hi-jacking, if I cannot let my wife walk alone down the street at night, if my house can be broken into by the gas company because my bill was lost by the Post Office, if I fear that my doctor may kill me when I become a burden; then by so much is my freedom curtailed.[47] If I am less free, then so is the rest of the community.

It is man's nature to live in communities, to trade, to work, to learn and teach. If a community is to enable the individual to grow, then he must be free. If there is to be freedom in any society, then basic duties must be fulfilled by all. It is evident, therefore, that the duties spring from the Nature of Man. They were not invented by Moses or King John's Barons. There are no communities in which they do not apply—anywhere on earth, any time in history. As Edmund Burke said :

"The principles that guide us, in public and in private, as they are not of our devising, but moulded into the nature and the essence of things, will endure with the sun and the moon—long, very long, after Whig and Tory, Stuart and Brunswick, and all such miserable bubbles and playthings of the hour, are vanished from existence and from memory."

Duties arise in many situations. If I hold a knife, I have a duty not to stab someone with it. If I borrow money, I have a duty to repay it. As I am a parent, it is my duty to feed my children. As I am a doctor, my duty is to restore my patients to health. Parliament has the duty to govern and defend the realm, the Trade Unions to defend the rights of their members. Always it is something owed to the weaker by the stronger. In the natural order of things the men to whom we owe the most, the ones who receive most, are therefore the weakest, the poorest and the humblest. Is this not what civilization is all about? Nature requires of us that we provide our best care, our greatest concern, our strongest protection, for the infant and for the senile and dying, because they cannot help themselves.

To fail to provide for the needs of the dying is to fail in a basic duty. The self-evident requirements of a dying man are to have his symptoms relieved, and to be allowed to die with dignity and peace of mind. If we evade all the difficult problems he presents, and just kill him, we have failed. Whether such euthanasia were voluntary or not is irrelevant : it is our duty so to care for these patients that they never ask for euthanasia. A patient who is longing to die is not being treated properly.[29] If we are not treating him properly, the solution is to improve our treatment, not to kill him. Is this not self-evident?

As it stood, Lord Raglan's Bill of 1969 gave inadequate definitions of who could and who could not request euthanasia. One does not, after all, want to make it easier for doctors to commit murder, or for depressed people to enlist assistance with suicide. But under the

Bill, a person could request to be killed if he had a "serious physical illness or impairment reasonably thought in the patient's case to be incurable and expected to cause him severe distress or render him incapable of rational existence."

Let us reflect on these provisions. It is simply not possible to decide which illnesses are physical, and which mental. Senility, for instance, has a physical basis in impairment of blood flow to the brain by hardening of the arteries which supply it. The patient with heart disease in his fifties could say he had an incurable illness very likely to cause him distress. Distress is so subjective—do we accept the patient's assessment of whether it is severe or not? If so, how could one exclude arthritis, asthma, psoriasis or even schizophrenia? There is no way of telling whether a patient's depression is pathological, or normal and reasonable in the circumstances. Where is the dividing line between rational and irrational existence?

All things considered, it would be hard to refuse anyone in late middle age and the Bill would have opened the door for death on demand. This may be what some of its advocates wanted, but I am sure it was not what the majority—including Lord Raglan—ever intended. The Bill was altogether unworkable, and Lord Raglan himself acknowledged this before retiring from the debate. He said in the London Medical Group conference on 5th February, 1972, that he could not envisage any Bill with adequate safeguards, and that anyway euthanasia would be unnecessary if terminal care all over the country were brought up to the standard he had seen in the hospices. Such a retraction by an eminent person takes great courage, and we can only admire Lord Raglan's "bold, just and impartial spirit."

Had the Bill been passed into law, it would have been the one and only exception to the old legal principle that the consent of the victim is no defence for the infliction of an injury. (Assault, for instance, is no less a crime if the victim is a masochist and requested or enjoyed the assault.)[42] As I mentioned on p. 84, surgical operations are justified by the legal doctrine of necessity, but euthanasia could not be. As Chancellor Garth Moore points out,* death for a man is, in the eyes of the law, a greater evil than pain, and so one could not say that a greater evil was averted by the deliberate killing of the patient.[16]

To admit into the Law the concept that some lives are not worth

* p. 50 of "Decisions about Life and Death"—see Bibliography.

living would be very dangerous. As the Abortion Act has crystallized a cheapening of the popular respect for human life, so would the passing of a euthanasia bill.[98, 111] The risk of abuse would be high, and another bale of straw would be on the camel's back, the camel being civilization itself.

Medical Considerations

Mrs. H. had a cancer of the womb. The surgeon was optimistic that he had successfully cured her, but a year later a lump could be felt again, and she looked ill. Rapidly her abdomen swelled up and some fluid was removed from it. The diagnosis was obvious : the cancer had recurred and was so widespread that the abdominal lining was being irritated so that it exuded the fluid. She came to the Hospice for terminal care. Every fortnight I relieved her abdominal distension by removing two or three gallons of fluid. She lost weight steadily. After several months the laboratory had been consistently unable to isolate malignant cells from the fluid, and Mrs. H. was still not dead. We began to wonder about the diagnosis. Eventually the surgeon agreed to do a further operation to see what was happening. The operation had the air of a mystery tour. What we found was a gigantic cyst on the ovary which filled her entire abdomen. Her weight loss was due to the great quantity of protein she lost in the fluid I was removing.

Mrs. H. is back at home leading a normal life.

What if the diagnosis of cancer (which made her depressed at first) had led to legal euthanasia? Mistaken diagnosis is a commonplace in medical practice.[28]

A lady who was sent to us with a brain tumour which had paralysed her right side had had an operation in which the surgeon had been unable to remove the growth. The diagnosis of a highly malignant "astrocytoma" was confirmed by looking at a piece of it under a microscope. The tumour continued to grow, producing a big lump on the side of her head. Her paralysis spread, her speech and vision were lost and she became incontinent. Her weight increased to about 18 stones. Drowsiness developed and progressed to coma. For a month she made little response at all to the daily visits of her devoted young husband. Then the lump went down. She woke up. The power of speech returned, and her limbs began to move. The physiotherapist set to work with delight, teaching her first to stand again, then to walk. The neurosurgeon assured

97

me that her recovery could only be temporary. A year after she came to us, he saw her again, and expressed surprise to me that she was still alive. He embarked upon further investigations. To everyone's astonishment there was no sign whatever of the tumour. She was rehabilitated and is now home again, her only residual disability being blindness, with which she can cope.

But that is not all. When the Hospice appeared on television, a conversation with this lady was broadcast. Several friends asked me "who that wonderful girl was?" She radiated an amazing joyfulness to everyone she met. The other patients adored her; to be reminded of her is uplifting. Her illness seemed to have been tailor-made to teach her something of profoundest significance.

What if her loss of consciousness had led to legal euthanasia?

I have another cautionary tale to tell of a boy of eight who made a miraculous recovery from a brain tumour which led to his transfer to the Hospice, unconscious. And in another hospice I knew a girl of sixteen with a malignant and painful sarcoma of the thigh bone which suddenly regressed, and has gone.

Last year a patient died of whom I was very fond. Mrs. L. had spent a good half of her seventy-nine years, including most of her childhood, in hospitals because she was born with dislocated hips. Adequate treatment was not known in those days and severe arthritis developed. In addition a war injury had left her totally bedbound. The arthritis caused unending and sometimes severe pain. When I first knew her she never smiled, and always grumbled. The bed, the nurses, her tablets, the food, me—everything was wrong, and she had innumerable minor complaints and symptoms. There was indigestion, sore mouth, severe itching, cataract in the eyes, sore throat, pain on movement, sinusitis and so on. On one occasion, she said to me "I wish I was in me box" and no wonder. Then an eminent rheumatologist saw her, and while he said that nothing could be done for her arthritis that we were not already doing, he diagnosed chronic depression and suggested that we should treat that.

The treatment worked wonders and Mrs. L. was urged to try some occupational therapy. Extra large needles that her deformed hands could grip were found, and some thick wool. She was cajoled into knitting me a scarf of great length. It was followed by bedjackets, blankets, another scarf and finally an exquisite tea cosy incorporating four different colours of wool. This latter was presented to us as a wedding present by a beaming Mrs. L. In fact she beamed at everyone and I found her surreptitiously reading a copy of *Lolita*. She still had the symptoms, but made light of them. They no longer filled the horizon because Mrs. L. had stopped paying attention to them. In her last few months of life she took the step of growing bigger than her body : so it ceased to be a trouble to her.

What if her unrelieved pain had led to a legal euthanasia, as she had once suggested? ✳

We admitted a Mr. N. with a very painful cancer, profoundly depressed. His wife had reacted to his illness with an anxiety state and his three teenage sons with resentment. He was very cut off. Gradually the boys came to terms with his condition and with a new picture of their father. Now he was no longer at home, his wife calmed down, and the boys started visiting. They found a new respect for their father in spite of his physical deterioration. With help from nurses and social workers, the whole family gradually came together again.

Had he been euthanased because of pain (which we controlled, of course) this could never have happened, and the rejecting family who agreed to the killing would have felt very guilty afterwards. Guilt is a common concomitant of grief, especially if the dead person committed suicide. What would the misery be like, afterwards, for relatives who had consented to the killing of their kin?

If anyone really wants euthanasia, someone must have failed him.

As I showed in the last chapter, it is not the duty of a doctor to produce candidates for euthanasia by administering inappropriate treatment to the senile and dying. Neither is there any need for the shortening of their life. Properly cared for, the potential candidate for the euthanasiast's needle will find new meaning in this very important part of life—for dying is still a part of living. In this period a man may learn some of his life's most important lessons. As I hope the above examples show, the "gap" of which Lord Dawson spoke (see p. 92 can be a very full one, and very productive.[186] Death need not be the final crushing defeat. On the contrary, a man can make a positive achievement of dying, a great final step forward.

Once a patient feels welcome, and not a burden to others : once his pain is controlled, and other symptoms have been at least reduced to manageable proportions, then the cry for euthanasia disappears.[200] It is not that the question of euthanasia is right or wrong, desirable or repugnant, practical or unworkable. It is just that it is irrelevant. Proper care is the alternative to it, and will be universally available as soon as there is adequate instruction of medical students in our teaching hospitals.[222] If we fail in this duty to care let us not turn to the politicians asking them to extricate us from the mess.

Mr. R. who was in a hospice for 5 weeks before he died, summed up the situation nicely : "A few days before I came here," he told me, "the pain got so bad that I was afraid I would die. By the time I got here, I was afraid I wouldn't. But now I'm here, I'm glad I didn't!"

> ". . . a mind fixed and bent upon somewhat
> that is good doth avert the dolours of death"
> Bacon[14]

Social Considerations

> The innocent and the just thou shalt not kill.
> —*Exodus*, 23.7

The Jewish-Christian tradition has stated this law, not as a theoretical standard, but because it is a basic requirement for the cohesion of civilized society.

Because of a lack of caring in our community some people die in distress. The same lack of caring leads people to suggest euthanasia as a solution. People are lonely, miserable and in pain because no one has troubled to relieve them. Euthanasia is suggested as the solution because still no one troubles to care. It would be an attractive easy option.[79]

The patient who was driven to ask for euthanasia would not be alone with his decision. The substance of our lives is in relationships with others. We are dealing with an interlocking community, not with isolated individuals. It follows that a law for individual relief should not be introduced until its social consequences have justified it.

To pass legislation permitting even a small number of doctors to kill some of their patients would be to introduce a whole new image for the medical profession—that of licensed killers.[113] If it accepted the legalization of euthanasia, society would expect the medical profession to help it to avoid the agony of looking after people who are seriously ill. It would affect the community's attitude to compassionate and constructive care of the elderly. It is a significant fact that there are no geriatricians among the Voluntary Euthanasia Society's membership at the time of writing.

At present, when one is sick, the hypodermic needle or the pain-killing draught are welcomed as a means of relief. But suppose it were possible that the needle or draught were not for relief, but to kill? Could trust survive? Such legislation would bring pressures on the old and ill to get themselves out of the way. It would be like saying to them, "If you cannot do anything you are worthless." The most considerate people would be the ones to suffer most. Whether loved or not, many would feel it encumbent upon them to request euthanasia because they did not wish to be a trouble to their family and friends. What of the slightly confused or forgetful old person who was not quite sure whether she had signed the paper or not? What of the person whose family wanted to be rid of him, and said so? Would you yourself not prefer euthanasia to going in to some of the old folks' homes in this country *in their present state*?

Were good care not possible at all, one would have to consider drastic alternatives. But since it certainly is possible and working examples abound, our efforts must be directed towards improving the attitude of society to the old and dying. We must rediscover and reaffirm their role in community life.

If we prefer the alternative—killing people (whether they ask for it or not)—we must contemplate the practicalities. If many doctors declined to kill patients (as is the case with abortion) there would arise special nursing homes for the purpose, with a doctor's fee. What should we call them? Disposal units? Thanatoria?

Consider the patient's relationships with his family. Usually no one would mention euthanasia or even death. But if they did, even from well-intentioned motives, a strain may be put on his relationships with them. Suppose a patient wanted euthanasia and his wife didn't agree (if she hid the signed form, Lord Raglan's Bill proposed a punishment of life imprisonment for her). Suppose half the family wanted the doctor to kill the patient and half did not. And what if a sister, say, discovered afterwards that the patient's wife had agreed. In short, would this legislation really reduce the sum of human suffering?

All things considered, do we really think that we have an improvement, in today's world, to replace our Christian moral code, our tradition of law and freedom, and our rich heritage of skill and knowledge? The principle of euthanasia, voluntary or involuntary, would run counter to Christian and Jewish morality; would limit our freedom by introducing a new fear for the elderly; and would misdirect the discoveries of science, which was properly intended for man's use in overcoming his adversities, not for evading them by instant death.

Even now the euthanasia lobbyists who are pressing for further discussions in Parliament are asking whether deformed children could not also be put to silence. Where will this end? Can an ancient and unbending moral law be superseded by what seems expedient and kind to well-meaning individuals? Where is the great Teacher who can redirect mankind into a better ethical code than that established by Christ, or Moses, or Buddha?[131]

If He is among the euthanasia lobby, let Him come and teach us.

Moral Considerations

"How long will ye give wrong judgement :
and accept the persons of the ungodly?
Defend the poor and fatherless :
see that such as are in need and necessity have right.
Deliver the outcast and poor :
save them from the hand of the ungodly.
They will not be learned nor understand,
but walk on still in darkness :
all the foundations of the earth are out of course.
I have said, Ye are gods :
and ye are all the children of the most Highest.
But ye shall die like men :
and fall like one of the princes."

Psalm 82 : 2–7 (Book of Common Prayer)

However a man may appear, there is reflected within him the highest and finest principle in the universe (how else could he speak of unity, of justice, or of love?). It may be thickly covered over, but it cannot be extinguished. For this reason the Quakers say "There is that of God in every man." That inner perfection can be served and respected in all men. There is no man who cannot receive love and be enriched by it. Good, sincere caring renders euthanasia unnecessary.

As the psalm suggests, it is man's nature to be immortal, constant and wise. The best law reflects these qualities. What the majority want is no basis for law. How can it be based on "public opinion" which alters daily? Such ethics spring from expediency, which is shifting and unreliable. This is why the great law-givers of our history have been followed and respected : they provided a code based on eternal principles more in accord with the nature of man. Moses did not invent the Ten Commandments any more than did Newton the law of gravity. They both simply gave expression to laws inherent in Nature.

The greatest law-givers saw that any relaxation of the rule forbidding one man to kill another would lead to social decline.[131] Lesser men, notably the Stoics,[62, 173] subsequently made all manner of exceptions to the rule : for "enemies," for criminals, for gladiators, for unborn babies, and finally, it is suggested, for the senile and suffering. All these exceptions are open to question. Society currently denies a man the "right" to euthanasia in order to conserve wider freedoms.[228]

Even from the individual's point of view, one must consider what a request for euthanasia really means. Is he trying to escape, to get away with something? Perhaps it is not possible to evade justice (hence the Roman Catholic doctrine of purgatory, and the Buddhist teaching of re-incarnation and Karma). Or is a man who requests euthanasia just uttering a cry for help? Should not a request for euthanasia alert us to reconsider the quality of our care for the person?

Suffering and death can never be eliminated from human experience, but the attitude of mind which wants to deny their existence and always to escape from them, can be overcome. Man can grow bigger than his troubles. With help, any man can do this—it is not just for the rare saint. I looked after a building foreman, for instance, who died sitting in an armchair. He had firmly refused bed for weeks, in spite of considerable shortness of breath, because he just wouldn't give in—he wanted to watch all that happened in the ward. I was filled with admiration, and the other men in his ward were filled with confidence, by his example.

Frequently the advocates of euthanasia refer to a "meaningless" or "useless" life.[56, 132] In my practical experience these descriptions can never be applied to human existence of any kind with certainty, and the moral theologian would point out that no life is meaningless in which any measure of self-realisation is still possible.[102] Without doubt it is in this sphere that the most muddled thinking goes on. In a letter to *The Times*, for instance, the Rev. Dr. Leslie Weatherhead wrote,

> "Those who condemn euthanasia on religious grounds seem to have lost their sense of logic. They say, 'leave it to God.' I would like to show them the parts of my garden that I have left to God!... We are to co-operate with God by using all available human help and we are to use our common sense. Man seeks to be the master of birth. He must just as sensibly seek to be the master of death. I would willingly give a patient Holy Communion and then remain while a doctor took measures to allow the patient to slip into the next phase of being while some degree of dignity remained."[234]

A few days later a doctor replied: "A medically qualified person is not needed. After all, our hangmen—and most murderers—were and are not medically qualified. With short instruction, any reasonably intelligent person could do the final act. People with sufficient sense of responsibility, such as lawyers and parsons, could be trained and appointed legal thanatophores. Dr. Weatherhead, for example, could administer Holy Communion, the Cup of Blessing, and then the coup de grace."[106]

The point to note in reply to Dr. Weatherhead is of course that "all available human help" for his garden would consist in pulling out the weeds of pain and despair, not blowing up the whole allotment.

Harestone Marie Curie Home, Caterham, Surrey

9

The Pains of Death

"IN birth there is pain, decay brings pain, disease is painful, death is painful."—So mused the Buddha in his famous sermon on the End of Suffering. But is all this pain really necessary?

Pain in the Body

Once again I will stress that for dying patients we should be treating symptoms, not diseases. Pain is the symptom we usually fear the most, particularly if we hear the much dreaded diagnosis of "cancer."[71] Indeed, without careful treatment 40% of patients with cancer might have severe pain.[225] Good treatment should anticipate pain, because if pain returns before the next dose of analgesics, it will be all the harder to control.[63] If they are given regularly, the dose of analgesics can be kept low,[148] though there should be no hesitation in giving sufficiently large doses.

I remember one old Glaswegian patient who found his own optimum dose. He came to us from one of H.M. Prisons, with the pain killers for his lung cancer in a sealed bag. He was a guest of H.M. for being drunk and disorderly, but the prison doctors had found that he had only a short time to live. In the ambulance he opened the medicines, and finding that one was liberally laced with gin he swigged from it with delight. On arrival he rather unsteadily handed me the empty bottle, and I realized with horror that he had consumed about fifteen times the normal dose of morphine. I watched to see if he would lapse into a coma, but all that arose was a happy smile and "Och, it sure got rid o' the pain, doc."

What must be avoided is the giving of analgesics "when necessary" (or "P.R.N." as doctors say, from the Latin *pro re nata*). This means that the pain gradually builds up until the patient asks a nurse for relief. She will tell the ward sister, who will have to break off from her other work to give an injection. The drug brings drowsiness with pain relief and the patient remains dully half-aware until he cries out again for morphine. Then someone says "I suspect he's getting addicted." For a dying patient, however, there is no maximum dose of an analgesic drug.

A Mr. H. told me he had been "in agony for three months." I thought he was romancing until I examined him with attention, and found how intensely tender were the cancer deposits in his ribs. Even breathing hurt him and any movement produced whimpers of misery from great pain. He had been receiving powerful opiate analgesics throughout three months, but the dose had been kept down for fear of addiction. Two days after coming to the Hospice he was sitting up, relaxed and smiling. Pain of the kind that Mr. H. had endured can seem to fill the whole universe leaving the patient conscious of little else.

If pain is properly controlled, the patient will never feel it again. He will ask if the medicines are really necessary any more, because the pain has gone.[188] Then it may be possible for him to return home and have his pain control organized as an outpatient.[181] In the clinic, medical and social support can be combined at the time when it is most needed and the patient can die comfortably at home.[182]

The opiates are not the only analgesics, of course. They can be very effectively supplemented by more homely remedies such as aspirin, rubs with oil of wintergreen three times a day,[225] and plenty of alcohol—which is a first class sedative and an excellent adjuvant in the relief of pain.[37] Such measures may be sufficient in themselves, but as Dr. C. J. Gavey pointed out,

"When observing patients with inoperable cancer, we can detect perhaps more clearly than in any other fatal disease, a fairly sudden change, from one day to the other; a change in both physical state and outlook arising from overwhelming weakness; a sign that the body has given up the struggle. From this point morphine should seldom be withheld and considerable pain will determine its even earlier use."[71]

Addiction can be avoided by the proper handling of these drugs.[37, 175] If the analgesic dose needed to control the pain is rising unduly, this is probably a sign that more sedatives or tranquilizers are needed. For pain is not simply a matter of electrical impulses travelling up particular nerves. It is an expression of the way the whole individual meets the events of his life.[61] Long-standing relentless pain is almost a disease in itself, because of the devastating effects it has on the person. He cannot get away from it, it commands his attention, and yet it seems completely meaningless. Dr. Lawrence LeShan likened the situation to a nightmare :

"The person in pain is in the same formal situation; terrible things are being done to him and he does not know if worse will happen; he has no control and is helpless to take effective action; no time limit is given . . . the patient lives during the waking state in the cosmos of the nightmare."[119]

Whether a person can be helped to *find* a meaning to his pain will be considered in the next chapter.

Exactly how, and why, we experience pain is obscure, and very complex.[184] We can colour it with what we fear it may be like in the future and what we remember of a previous pain (do you remember the dentist saying "But I haven't touched you yet!"?). A great deal of distress can be relieved if the patient sees that doctors and nurses tackle it with enough confidence, and in emergency pain may not be felt at all, as has often been noted on the battlefield.[20]

Everything which causes physical discomfort has to be dealt with : sore mouths and painful infections like boils and cystitis, for instance. Insomnia is also distressing. Sleeping tablets may be a help (with the exception of barbiturates which may lead to confusion and incontinence in debilitated or elderly folk) but it is necessary to enquire into the cause of the sleeplessness. Perhaps it is due to pain, which is often worse at night. In this case the analgesics have to be given regularly right round the clock, with a slightly higher dose at night.[89] A cough can also make sleep impossible, so a linctus should be available at the bedside. One of the worst enemies of sleep is anxiety. Alcohol or sedatives may have a place here, but nothing compares with a sympathetic listener. Then there are the obvious causes of insomnia that can easily be overlooked. If the patient is at home the person with whom he sleeps may be restless. If he is in hospital other patients may be noisy or the bed may be hard.

Patients with brain tumours may suffer with severe headaches and nausea due to pressure from fluid collecting round the tumour. This pain can be managed with "physics, chemistry and biology" : the fluid pressure can be lowered by raising the head of the bed by 20–25 centimetres (8–10 inches) and providing a "donkey" (see p. 54) to prevent him from sliding down the bed; a diuretic drug may be given which makes the patient pass more urine thus lowering the fluid pressure in all his cells by chemical means; and from the biological angle the activities of the cells themselves may be modified by large doses of steroid drugs (up to 4 mg. Dexamethasone, thrice daily). Smaller doses of steroids (5 mg. Prednisone, thrice daily) can relieve the widespread aches and pains and the loss of appetite from which dying patients often suffer.[226]

Two of the most distressing symptoms are constipation (see p. 54) and, perhaps the worst of all, breathlessness. If this is not controlled (see p. 36 and 47), it can lead to extreme anxiety and panic.[63] The physical and mental suffering are closely interwoven, and this division into bodily and mental pains is clearly an artificial one. What has to be considered when treating pain, is just how the patient sees it, not what an outside observer makes of it. If the patient says it is agonising, that is the assessment that really counts because no one else can share his way of experiencing it.[51]

Pain in the Mind

Many physical symptoms produce, or may be the result of, characteristic attitudes of mind. Anxiety, as has been said, accompanies breathlessness, and depression comes with nausea, weakness or loss of appetite. When the strain of keeping a stiff upper lip proves too great—as it usually does—[232] humiliation can result. Not that disease itself can be humiliating—it cannot, because humiliation is a particular relationship between people. Things cannot be humiliating, only people can. Good nursing manifests respect for the patient, and preserves his dignity whatever happens.

A host of fears assail dying people which we can detect if we are sensitive. There is the fear of further mutilating operations and uncomfortable treatments, for instance. This is often the answer to an astonished "But why didn't you come earlier?" when someone approaches the doctor for the first time with disease which has progressed hopelessly beyond a curable stage.

Often people have the most bizarre and frightening ideas about their diseases. One man with cancer of the stomach had a sore throat, and I discovered that he was afraid it was the cancer spreading up from below to strangle him. There are patients who will not go to sleep in case they die, or worse are thought to be dead, and then buried alive. Many people fear that they will be sent mad by a cancer, that it is infectious or hereditary or just dirty and disgusting. All these fears are groundless and, once unearthed, they can be dispelled.

A Mrs. G. told us that it had been more frightening suspecting that she was dying than it was actually to know. In this uncertainty all manner of terrors can lurk, particularly the fear that when death itself comes it will be violent, with severe pain or suffocation.[121] In fact we find that pain nearly always subsides just before the end, that the patient feels only an overwhelming drowsiness and dies in his sleep. All these fears are ghosts which can be exorcised by anyone who will discuss them or refer them to the doctor.[246] You can hear in a person's voice if these fears are there. A Miss P. whose bowel cancer had been by-passed by a colostomy,* and who had lost two stones in weight, said to me as I examined her abdomen, "There doesn't seem to be much wrong does there, doctor?" There was such questioning in this cautious probe that I sat down to listen. "I don't understand about this colostomy," she went on. "Is it going to heal up?" A patient should never be left with this kind of uncertainty.

Some patients are very resentful of a disability which they feel is being imposed on them. They will blame the hospital, or the drugs, or the doctors. For many people the idea of becoming dependent on others is unbearable. They need very matter-of-fact help, the worst of all things for them being pity, which implies a lower status.[119]

* A hole made in the abdomen wall through which bowel motions empty into a bag. It may be closed in a later operation, or may be permanent.

Under this kind of stress, some people regress to childish behaviour. One can make allowances for this if it is understood as a defence-reaction to a situation they cannot bear to face. While he is strong enough, a person with this kind of personality will want all the physiotherapy and rehabilitation possible,[53, 55] particularly if he can make or do something useful for other people.[15] Later, when dependence on others is thrust on him, nurses should remember not to chat to one another as if he were not there, doctors should not discuss his case over him, and everything done to him should be carefully explained beforehand.[104]

A rather different kind of person will react to severe disease with intense grief. Suppose a hostile government were to announce that you had contravened a law that you had forgotten ever existed, and as a punishment stripped you of house and job and banished you. Family and friends would be lost forever behind an iron curtain. This is how some people feel when they are dying. The relatives who remain alive are only losing one person, but the dying man is losing everything :[7, 36] his wife, his garden, the dog, his favourite chair and his own body.

"If only I could spend just a few days at home, in my little garden; it must be very beautiful now the spring is here." So said Mrs. R. who was completely bedridden. The pain from her cancer could only be controlled by an injection every four hours, supplemented by other analgesics given by mouth in between the injection times. She had thoroughly enjoyed her retirement, her home and her friends, and was very reluctant to lay them aside.

Another lady was miserable shortly after her last Christmas at home. I asked her what was depressing her. She cried a little and said, "Nothing really, it's silly." I said it was not silly, or she would not be crying. It transpired that she wanted just one more look at home. This was a tall order because she was too weak to get out of a chair, and was bleeding internally. However, I agreed to make plans for the projected trip and we fixed a day. Then I asked again what was depressing her. She clenched her fists and said "If I am ... ill ... again, can I come back here?" Her greatest pain was bereavement, but her greatest fear was loneliness.

This estrangement from the world haunts many people as they die, and they will try to compensate for it in various ways if they are not befriended. They may become overdemanding for fear of being left alone. They may complain vociferously about relatively minor pains as a respectable way of attracting attention.[182] It is always worth while asking yourself, when somebody complains of pain, whether he is trying to communicate some other need to you as well.[89, 119] Careful listening to the complaint will reveal if this is so. Loneliness is particularly likely to produce this "social pain" in a patient,[183] and so is worry about how the family will manage without him.[225] Thus it can be seen that the social worker and the occupational therapist have a part to play in the relief of pain.

It is vital to maintain some kind of social life right to the end, for facing the unknown alone and friendless is a frightening prospect. One lady in a hospice said to me "You can talk to people more here. There everybody walked away from me." When we do not walk away we share some of the pain. We may not understand, we cannot prevent the hard thing that is happening, but what really counts to the dying person is that someone cares enough to try. This was well expressed by Dr. Ronald Welldon, shortly before his own death :

"... as the realistic hopes of curative treatment diminish, the human or personal factors of relationship, motivation and emotion assume an importance which may not have been so obvious at a more optimistic stage. It becomes so much more tolerable to face intolerable aspects of a disease process, of oneself, and of life, if one can do so in the company of at least one other person, who is himself prepared to share something of this intolerability. Such a person does not necessarily have to hold a medical degree, but it helps. The person in the best position to help is still most frequently the family doctor, who has ready access to the patient as a member of a particular social group, with its various resources."[237]

The last of the mental pains which will be considered in this section is guilt. On a superficial level this can be felt by a patient who is incontinent or has a discharging ulcer which has a bad smell. The bed linen should be frequently changed, and the patient frequently reassured that those nursing him don't mind doing this. Infected ulcers can be treated remarkably effectively by injections of a mixture of penicillin and streptomycin,* provided that the

---

* Crystamycin : one vial twice daily for about five days, until the smell subsides, then maintain on one dose per day.

patient is not so thin that the injections are too painful. The ulcers themselves can be rinsed or syringed clean with the solutions recommended for deep bedsores on p. 53, and the use of yoghurt as a dressing prevents further infection.

At a deeper level, a man may be burdened with feelings of guilt or incompleteness on looking back over a mediocre life. The disease may feel like a punishment. When one lady was told that she was dying she said, "I get so depressed you know: I've never done anyone any harm."

Oddly enough, psychotherapists are very cautious about relieving people of this guilt, as we shall see in the next chapter, for it has in it an element of truth.

Some people seem to know instinctively that there need not be any pain, while others face it and rise above it so that they can watch it with relative indifference. A Belgian lady, shortly before her demise, said to me with a twinkle, "I am pleased to die." Another patient, Mr. P., whose pain was needing larger doses of analgesics than are usual, and who was very breathless because cancer had destroyed most of his lung, insisted on cutting down his night sedation so as to be more alert in the mornings. "I'm not throwing the towel in," he said, "I'm going to win just one more fight—last it out a bit anyway!"

Dr. Cicely Saunders wrote:

"Dependence on others is not the worst evil that can happen to us, and there are tremendous possibilities in accepting and sharing. Suffering is part of the whole of life, and although I spend my whole time trying to relieve it, I know what gains it brings to patient and family alike and what an immense deepening there so often is in their relationships."[198]

The Greatest Pain of All

Being in a position to relieve these pains, mental and physical, and to enable people to face death and be enriched by the experience in their own way as Mr. P. did, makes one feel very humble. What is even more humbling is to realize that there is another pain, which we cannot treat, afflicting ourselves as well as our patients. It is bound up with our common mortality. Physical pains we suffer alone; mental pains, particularly grief, affect the whole circle of our acquaintances. But the greatest pain of all, a pain of the spirit, is as great as mankind. It is the pain of a prodigal son.*

Your pain is the breaking of the shell that encloses your understanding.

Even as the stone of the fruit must break, that its heart may stand in the sun, so must you know pain.

And could you keep your heart in wonder at the daily miracles of your life, your pain would not seem less wondrous than your joy;

And you would accept the seasons of your heart, even as you have always accepted the seasons that pass over your fields.

And you would watch with serenity through the winters of your grief.

Much of your pain is self-chosen.

It is the bitter potion by which the physician within you heals your sick self.

Therefore trust the physician, and drink his remedy in silence and tranquility :

For his hand, though heavy and hard, is guided by the tender hand of the Unseen.

Kahlil Gibran : *The Prophet* (Heinemann, London, 1967)

* Luke, 15 : 11–32.

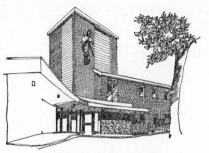

St. Luke's Nursing Home, Sheffield

10

Counselling the Dying

> Oh why do people waste their breath
> Inventing dainty names for death?
> Sir John Betjeman—*Churchyards.*

AT his best, Man has no fear of death. The function of psycho-therapy is simply to remind a man who he is. Our present-day con-spiracy to ignore death looks like a community-sized act of cowardice. As Katharine Whitehorn said, "Somehow we've got to get death back into the conversation, stop sheltering children from any faintest contact with it; work out what things we would die for, the things without which we would not care to go on living."[240]

Miss K., a Polish music teacher who knew that she was dying, commented one day on her weakness and drowsiness. The conversa-tion developed as follows :

"The weakness is due to your anaemia."

"Aren't the tablets dealing with that?"

"They will help, but they can't really stop it. If we were to replace the lost blood by a blood transfusion into a vein in your arm, that would bring it back to normal. Would you like that?"

"What would happen then? Would I be cured?"

"Oh no. It would make you feel better, but you would have to go through the same process once more as the anaemia developed again. But it would mean that you would live a little longer."

"I think I would prefer to be left in peace. . . . I am not afraid to die," Miss K. continued, "and I thank you very much, doctor, for giving me this warning, for taking the first step in preparing me for the long journey ahead." When I left her, she was looking . . . joyful? imperial? anyway quite awesome. Her peace and strength never faltered until she died six weeks later.

Miss K. was well prepared to die, but in general people pretend that no such thing could ever happen, and they will need to be brought to acceptance gradually. Metropolitan Anthony (Archbishop Anthony Bloom) described his dismay and horror at the prevalent attitude to death which he found on coming to England : "I belong to a nation and to a Church (Russian Orthodox) where death is considered as part of life. Death is a normal thing—a function of man to face—and one of the things I met in this country is that death is almost an indecency. People shouldn't do that to their friends ! And if they fall so low as to do it, generally one turns to specialists who can deal with the problem. That is, the dead person is left in a corner until the undertakers come and do what is to be done, after which the family and friends at best are confronted with the coffin. . . ."[23]

It is fascinating to notice how different people come to accept death. A Mrs. L., three weeks before she died, became suspicious of her failure to recover :

"I'm not making any headway am I?"

"Not at the moment," I said.

"When I had the operation for the cancer in my stomach. . . . I suppose it was a cancer, wasn't it. . .?"

"Yes."

". . . I wonder if they left a bit behind?"

"It could be connected with that."

"So I'll have to grin and bear it."

For some days Mrs. L. was difficult to nurse and then declared that as we could do nothing for her, she was going home. Her family came to us in panic—there was no one to nurse her at home, how could she go? She sullenly listened to me as I tried to reason with her, and finally agreed to sleep on it. The next day a completely different Mrs. L. greeted me with a grin and said "All right, I've settled." She was cheerful for the whole of her last week.

A dour Irish labourer, Mr. D., made his peace with death in a way that disrupted a whole ward. When he found out that he was dying, he went into a huff and refused all medicines. He assailed me one morning with :

"Doctor ! This is unsufferable."

"Why ?"

"It's very painful. Couldn't I be examined at the London Hospital again ?"

"There's nothing anyone can do to heal it, I'm afraid."

"I want to see a specialist."

"You already have, and he sent you to us. If you have pain, it's your own fault : you refused the medicine."

"I'm having no more medicine."

"Then you'll have pain."

"There's gin in the medicine," interjected Sister, offering him the analgesic mixture. He wavered a moment, then drank it with gusto, raising the glass aristocratically.

"They told me it was a widespread cancer," he said.

"Yes," I confirmed.

"So I'm not long here? Soon I'll be up there. And I'm ready to go." (raising his voice) "Death where is thy sting? GRAVE WHERE IS THY VICTORY?"

I retreated.

In all such conversations the patient leads the way. The achievement is his, and the role of the caring team is only to watch for impediments which may disturb his peace of mind. Some will never come to terms with their fate, demanding reassurance to the last. "They must be allowed their choice. They find their own way through and it seems clear to me that one does not necessarily have to know that death is imminent to be well prepared to meet it. Trust and faith in life and in death are not so very different."[189]

Mr. H. was a patient who made it clear that no further discussion would be appropriate. On arrival at the Hospice, he said to me "As far as I know I've been sent here for convalescence. That's as far as I know." Clearly he *did* know that he was very ill, but was not yet ready to face the fact.

It is not a case of what to tell a patient, but of what we will let him tell us.[191] We must just listen. Then the patient will give all the cues, however brief the conversation. When that little probing half-question comes up—"That lump's bigger, isn't it? : I think the paralysis is spreading, nurse : I can't hold my cup these days"; and such like—when the question comes up—then we can be ready to recognize it and give a few minutes of honest listening. Tiredness, overwork or being in a rush, can never be an excuse for refusing to give this inestimable help.[40] If we really listen, then these little conversations do not usually take long, for time is not a question of length, it is a question of depth.

Even when dying, a person can still have a sense of purpose and self-esteem. The mode of dying will be as individual as the person himself. I even knew one lady who told us the date of her death a week in advance. She had been told in a dream that she would meet her dead sister again on Friday-the-Thirteenth. On the twelfth she looked so well that we joked about it, but the next day, having deteriorated suddenly, she announced that she would soon die. And she did.

A Mr. D. wondered if he would reach his next birthday which was three weeks away. "Yes," I said, "but not the next one." He smiled and said "Good : I don't want to."

A Mrs. G. said to a hospice doctor, "I'm getting weaker. Can't you do anything about it?"

"Not at the moment," he replied.

"So I shall just get weaker and weaker?"

"You could also get happier and happier."

"I know." She smiled and relaxed; "I've had a happy life."

In this way a person's whole attitude can be deftly turned to bring out what is positive in them. However it is not always such plain sailing, and some patients will need more of the counsellor's time. If we are to help, we first need to realize that seriously ill patients *will* have considered the possibility of death.[40] Professor Hinton found that nearly three quarters of a group of dying patients had a good idea that they were dying. Of those, one quarter thought that they might possibly die, a half thought that they were probably dying, and the rest knew that they were.[94] Yet in Britain half of the family doctors never tell a patient that he is dying, and 96% tell less than half of them. In America 96% of doctors do not usually tell anyone that he will soon die.[72]

This failure to communicate is largely a failure to listen, which is itself the principal therapy. Patients may experience great relief just from being able to unburden themselves of fears, grief, feelings of guilt and failure, of loneliness or of frustration at being so dependent on others. Sharing such feelings can be consoling for the patient, though rather uncomfortable for the listener. To render this service, we have to be prepared to be disturbed.[22] By listening to a patient one can redirect his attention from his symptoms or worries, on to the topic being discussed. Alternatively one might enable him to bring some of his worst fears and suspicions out into the light of consciousness, where they will lose much of their strength. Emotions seen and understood are manageable, particularly if the patient can be reassured that they are not his guilty secrets, but the sort of thing everyone feels in such circumstances.[119] Fear that there will be pain can be countered with confidence.

The value of the companionship of a listener to dying people is delightfully described in a letter written by the philosopher Epictetus on the day of his death :

> "On this truly happy day of my life, as I am at the point of death, I write this to you. The diseases in my bladder and stomach are pursuing their course, lacking nothing of their usual severity; but against all this is the joy in my heart at the recollection of my conversation with you."

Sometimes there will be very little to be said. Mrs. K., a doughty old cockney, countered my probing questions with "I know I've got something wrong with me," and changed the subject. Just before she died, with the family all sitting around the bed she fixed me severely with her eye and said, "I'm just going to sleep, that's all."

Denial, Dependence, Transference and Regression

The first thing people do with bad news is to sweep it under the carpet.

Mr. L., a young family man with cancer of the rectum, said to me, "Cor, this pain's killing me. Can't you do something about it?"

"Yes," I said, "we can control the pain."

"Oh good, because my little lad's coming in this afternoon, and I don't want him to see me in this state. Blimey."

Sometime later, after an injection of diamorphine, Mr. L. asked me how long he would be in the Hospice.

"I don't want to be off work too long. That injection did the trick. Thanks very much. I feel I could get up now—will that be all right? I don't want the family to think I'm bedbound!"

Despite severe pelvic pain and considerable loss of weight, Mr. L. had returned to work after an exploratory operation and now felt extremely ill. His refusal to come to terms with his illness was cutting him off from everyone. The wall of optimism which he strenuously erected around himself made sympathy difficult, especially when he never even waited for answers to his questions. That he was obviously fearful of possible answers showed that subconsciously he knew his prognosis, but he was certainly not yet able to receive the concrete confirmation of his fears. Indeed, we had one lady with us who asked her diagnosis on three separate ward rounds, and each time denied having been told before; such was her refusal to face what she well knew. Because we meet this situation so frequently we have come to regard it as a normal development. This wall of denial is like the battlements of a mediaeval castle, where guards are ever vigilant, protecting the person until the moment when he is ready to face the truth.

"My wife's dead, most of my friends are dead, there's nothing left to hold me. I wouldn't mind if I were to die tomorrow." This more aged patient spoke for the majority of his generation. They are usually willing to go. But a few have difficulty with adjusting to the situation, and may need more skilled counselling.

A relatively common reaction when a person first begins to realize that a cure is not possible, is anger. Quite a simple idea may be at the root of it, such as "How dare my body let me down?" or "Why can't this doctor stop playing about, and heal me?" or "But I *must* look after the children until they have left school." If the patient is very polite it may all come to the surface as an anxiety state, but usually he will direct the anger against some particular person or hospital. The counsellor can help him to see what the answer is really about, always bearing in mind that some of it is probably quite justified. The most valuable help at such a time is a stable reliable person who can ride the storm—a "father figure" as the jargon has it. The person usually most fitted for this role is the family doctor,[4] though problems arise if the patient needs him, but is seen instead by a relief service doctor. The presence of such a supporting person, or group of people, brings the patient a great sense of safety.

It is part of man's nature to live in families. Throughout our lives our relationships with others reflect the original relationships in our early family life. In emotionally charged situations we may "transfer" the full strength of our feelings of love or repulsion for childhood companions to the people caring for us. Criticism of, and undue involvement with the patient can often be avoided if the staff understand this. Occasionally it helps the patient to be given some insight into these reactions. Only a skilled counsellor should embark on this, however, lest some precious relationship be upset when there is not time enough for the patient to rebuild it. The intensity of this transference of feelings is likely to be directed at the counsellor himself, and so Professor Cramond[40] stressed that the same counsellor should support the patient through to the end, otherwise the patient may suffer an additional bereavement.

Another series of reactions which may be set off can be particularly exasperating for the nurses. It is called "regression." As more and more has to be done for the patient he becomes as dependent as a baby. Understandably his behaviour may become correspondingly childish. He may thus be defiant and rebellious in an effort to reassert his lost independence, or annoyingly demanding. The staff tend to reject such a patient, which makes him all the worse, or they may be mothering and indulgent, which an intelligent patient will resent.

Mrs. G., for instance, a lady of seventy-seven with cancer of the tongue which had spread to the glands in her neck, asked me one day, "What's this lump in my neck?"

"It's just the same as the one on your tongue," I replied evasively.

"Whatever that is," she parried, "I know you won't tell me."

"Of course I will, if you want me to."

"What is it then? It is a cancer isn't it?"

"Yes, but it's all confined to this small area."

"I've asked before several times," she said, "I told them I was old enough to know! . . . Thank you. I'll just keep smiling and put up with it then." Whereupon she smiled, splendidly.

Some people, in coming to terms with a grave prognosis, try to bargain for time. One man who said he wanted to put his affairs in order asked me his diagnosis. "It won't upset me," he said, "whatever you tell me." The word cancer was not used, but he was told his body was wearing out fast and would never be strong again. He asked how long he had left. I said I did not know, but it was probably only a few months. "But I might hang on for a couple of years perhaps, would you say?" He said he would be willing to die, provided he could just have a holiday in the country first.

Another patient asked each member of the medical staff what his prognosis was, trying to find someone who would make a lengthy forecast. Three days before he died, however, there was a total change. He compared dying to going to a new school—"an alarming change, but pleasant in retrospect!"

Many people respond to the knowledge of impending death with depression, particularly when they have pain which has not been properly controlled. Endless meaningless pain wears a person down, "weakens his ego" as the saying goes, because there is no appropriate response to it, no apparent meaning in it. A counsellor may help the patient to discover a meaning in his suffering—something meaningful to the patient, that is, not necessarily to the counsellor—and as Dr. LeShan says,

> "It is perhaps important for the therapist first to be clear about his own feelings in this area before he can effectively help the sufferer. If he believes that there is a meaning, even if he cannot find it, he is in a much better position to help."[119]

I have a friend with multiple sclerosis with which he copes admirably, using a wheelchair and Possum typewriter. He frequently meets people as ill as himself or worse, and is a constant source of encouragement to them because they see how one man copes with overwhelming problems. He sees this as his role, and thus wrests advantages out of the disease itself.

A depressed patient will worry about unfinished jobs in the past or anticipated suffering and bereavement in the future. He can be reassured by stressing what he did achieve, what his life has stood for, and by being told that death will be peaceful. Indeed, if he is in a hospice with other dying patients he will see this for himself. If he feels that he is a nuisance to others at home, he can be told that his family really want him there. If he is in hospital it can be pointed out to him that the nurses and doctors only chose their kind of work because they wanted to help nuisances. However, guilty feelings should not all be dismissed and reassured away, even if that were possible. Guilt, and any pain or other "conversion symptom" to which it gives rise, may be felt by a patient to be an atonement, a penance, without it he may feel that his values have gone, leaving him aimless. To quote Dr. LeShan's paper again :

> "The question should be asked : 'Is there a purpose behind this pain in this particular patient?' 'Does it hold off guilt?' 'Does it provide him with a sense of being real that he desperately needs?' 'Is it a conversion symptom and, if so, of what?' One ignores these questions at the risk of successfully answering the patient's conscious plea for relief and destroying his adjustment."

None of these moods and attitudes will be fixed. If one looks afresh at a patient during each visit, he will be seen to fluctuate between being dignified and capable, and childishly dependent. He may behave regressively while being bathed, but responsibly when writing his will. If his dignity is to be maintained, some means of formally expressing his independence should be provided. He may be able to share in the doctor's decisions about his treatment; if he is capable of making things in occupational therapy, an opportunity should be provided for him to sell these to help provide for his family or to give to charity. Any "when necessary" drugs could be given into his care; he could choose his meals from a daily menu, and keep his own photographs, ornaments or cards on a bedside locker so that his bed area bears the distinct stamp of his personality.[140] As long as he is able to, a dying man should manage his own affairs and be consulted on family problems. A policy of "don't trouble him with that now, he's ill" will only worsen his feeling of isolation.

Some sort of support system is essential to deal with problems which arise as a patient swings between being dependent and self-sufficient. The person who gives this support should not usually be the one who does the nursing and the cooking, because this will only accentuate his dependent status. A complete outsider is more suitable, preferably a social worker, psychotherapist or psychiatrist. His visits can also provide support for the caring team as well as for the patient, especially if rebellion in a patient is being projected on to other people or the institution caring for him. The staff can share with the counsellor any feelings of aggression towards a patient, or of bereavement if a favourite one dies.

These various patterns of interaction between people, and between patients and their environment, can give rise to difficulties which can be very absorbing to treat. They are, however, only mechanical malfunctions of the mind, and no more a substitute for the man himself than his body is. It is easy to suppose that, having mastered psychology, one has understood Man; but there is much more to see than these paintings on his shell.

Support at the End

The dying need regular and frequent visits[182] to show that interest is still being taken in them. Above all they must be assured that whatever happens they will not be deserted. At least one of the team should be with the family to support them throughout the terminal period, otherwise they would have no one in whom to place their confidence. This can be the social worker,[46] nurse[136] or family doctor.[37] If this person calls while the patient is asleep, he should at least leave a note to say that he called.

The patient should be helped not to put things off "until I feel better," and not to hold back from emotional contact with others on the same pretext.[121] He may need to be reassured that the end will not be long now, and that someone will be with him at the hour of his death.

"I have known several who wanted to talk only a few hours before they died. They were not frightened nor unwilling to go, for by then they were too far away to want to come back. They were conscious of leaving weakness and exhaustion rather than life and its activities. They no longer had any pain but felt intensely weary. They wanted to say goodbye to those they loved but were not torn with longing to stay with them."—Dr. Cicely Saunders, in *Care of the Dying* (See Bibliography).

Finally we should remember that, since dying is a unique experience in each life, the man who is dying rightly expects some special consideration and indulgence.[155] Even those of us who see dozens of people die need to remember that what is familiar for us, is for the patient his biggest adventure.

St. Barnabas' Home, Worthing

11

Grief

They that love beyond the world cannot be separated by it.
Death cannot kill what never dies. Nor can spirits ever be
divided, they love and live in the same divine principle; the
root and record of their friendship.—From *Union of Friends*
by William Penn.

PART of care of the dying is care of the bereaved : they are two sides
of the same coin.

It is important to understand that grief begins from the moment
when a member of the family is told that the patient will not
recover. As soon as a person realizes that a part of his life is soon
to be torn away, a long process of grief begins which develops in
recognizable stages. As a process of healing and replacement, it
has been observed to involve work which the bereaved person has
to do on himself. Other people can help, but there is no avoiding
or sidestepping the process. As Helen Deutsch expressed it, "the
process of mourning as reaction to the real loss of a loved person
must be carried to completion"[49] and some authorities consider that
this applies even if the grief is suppressed or delayed by sedatives.

There has been remarkably little research into bereavement, and many questions, particularly in relation to bereaved children, are still unanswered. There is controversy over many of the points mentioned in this chapter. All I can do is to present the findings and theories of a few prominent workers in the field.

The effort involved in grieving has been divided into "worry work" before the loved person dies, and "grief work" afterwards. The way some of this work can be done before the death could be clearly seen in the parents of a teenager who died with us some years ago. They spent all their spare time with him in the ward, alert to his every need, fussing the nurses, questioning the doctors. His mother adjusted his pillows, straightened his sheets, tidied his locker and made him drinks almost incessantly. His father would show us photographs of the boy just before his illness had disfigured him. "This is the real Dick," he would say. "This is how he really looks." These parents were thus much more ready for the death when it came than they would have been had they not started grieving beforehand, though of course when the end came, it was still a crushing experience for them.

Another couple took home a brother with a brain tumour so that his care could be supervised by the out-patients department of the Hospice. The sitting room became a sick bay, and the other members of the family took turns in sitting with him at nights. They devised ways of enabling him to sit up and eat in spite of paralysis, and of communicating when he lost the power of speech. As he lapsed into unconsciousness they began to give away his various treasures and handicrafts, as if parting from him bit by bit.

The way in which grief begins before the death was described by a man who knew his wife would never leave the Hospice. "It's like a desert at home without her," he said. For this reason, no relatives should be told of a grave prognosis and then left to their own devices : they should at the same time be invited to come back and talk over their distress and questions. They will have so many decisions to make : Who should tell the patient that he is dying, and when? Should his house be sold? Should his son be recalled from Australia? How can he be asked to write a will? and so on. If the relatives are very upset and disorganized, they should be given something positive to do for the patient. For instance, they could be taught nursing procedures, or help with bathing or feeding a very weak patient.[207] This approach also helps people to get over the feelings of guilt which are often a part of grieving, as I shall explain later. Other relatives should be involved as much as possible, for it is the whole family which is bereaved, and together they can face it much better than each could alone.[78]

Often a family will look for a scapegoat to blame for their misfortune. They may be angry—with God, with the hospital or with individual members of the caring team. Doctors and nurses have to learn to accept this hostility without reacting. Arguing is no help : what is needed is understanding and a willingness to share their burden of misery.[246] This is possible if they are simply encouraged to talk and then listened to carefully. Often a clergyman is the best person for this kind of support, and should be introduced to the family as early as possible in the course of the patient's terminal illness.[13]

Gradually the time will approach for saying goodbye, which should not be omitted. One husband confided "I know she must be worrying about me but she doesn't talk of it. I would so much like to tell her that I will manage when she is gone." In this particular case the staff were able to break the ice for the couple, enabling them to share all their fears and hopes.

As the last hours approach, relatives may feel lonely. They will probably want to spend a lot of time with the patient, yet will need frequent attention and reassurance themselves. Comfortable chairs at the bedside, drinks and even meals should be provided. If they are obviously tired it can be suggested that they go and get some rest—in an adjoining quiet room if possible. Some will want to be with the patient at the moment of death, others would prefer not to be. Neither course should be favoured or criticized by the staff, but rather reinforced by assurance that it is the right course for them, and by affording them every help. It helps if they can be given some idea of how soon the death will come, what the medicines or injections are for, and if they are told that the staff will not allow any suffering to disturb the patient's sleep.

When the death does occur, it will be a shock for the relatives, however well-prepared they may be. One of the most helpful people at this point may be the undertaker,* getting on with his arrangements with quiet sympathy. But the relatives will need skilled support for much longer than he can offer it. When someone dies in hospital, therefore the family doctor and the parish priest should be informed at once, so that they can mobilize help, particularly

* Mortician in the U.S.A.

if the bereaved person has been left living alone. The family doctor should visit frequently,[4] and the clergyman should call in during the second week after the bereavement, and then periodically over the first year. A social worker should also be brought in to advise on the handling of insurance claims, death grants, widow's pensions, deeds of probate and so on.

Normal grief generally proceeds through a series of predictable stages, though each individual will work through his own variation of the pattern.[25]

At first, for a few days, only occasionally for more than a week, the person behaves almost as if nothing has happened. He handles day to day affairs like an automaton, feeling numb and empty. One lady whose mother had just died was stopped by a neighbour in the street.

"Good morning, E., how's your mother?"

"Oh she's fine thanks," came the reply, with a vacant smile.

After this numbness the pangs of grief begin. It is as though the person denies the fact of the death to himself, and experiences intense yearning to be reunited with the dead person.[161] The mind searches for the lost companion, only to be painfully frustrated again and again. These feelings are all the more violent if the death was sudden and unexpected so that no proper "worry-work" could be done.[219]

Dr. Erich Lindermann described such pangs as

"distress occurring in waves lasting from twenty minutes to an hour at a time, a feeling of tightness in the throat, choking with shortness of breath, need for sighing and an empty feeling in the abdomen, lack of muscular power, and an intense subjective distress described as tension or mental pain."[123]

Between these attacks

"the bereaved person is depressed and apathetic with a sense of futility. Associated symptoms are insomnia, anorexia, restlessness, irritability with occasional outbursts of anger directed against others or the self, and preoccupation with thoughts of the deceased. The dead person is commonly felt to be present and there is a tendency to think of him as if he were still alive and to idealize his memory. The intensity of these features begins to decline after one to six weeks and is minimal by six months, although for several years occasional brief periods of yearning and depression may be precipitated by reminders of the loss."[159]

Illusions of the presence of the dead person are common and normal, and may continue to occur at intervals for a decade or so. Some 50% of bereaved people in a Welsh study experienced these illusions of a dead spouse, and in Japan 90% of people did.[177] He may be seen sitting in his accustomed place, or heard to call the person's name, or to come in through the front door at the accustomed time each day. These experiences have also been recorded when the person is only thought to be dead, but in fact turns up again later, as happened frequently with prisoners of war for instance. It is therefore unlikely that they represent any real ongoing relationship with the dead.

Since these phenomena spring from an inner denial of the death, they are to some extent treasured by the person experiencing them. If others try to comfort him, thereby implying confirmation of the death, their efforts may be resented. Dr. John Bowlby says

"Thus, we see, repeated disappointment, weeping, anger, accusation, and ingratitude are all features of the first phase of mourning and are to be understood as expressions of the urge to recover the lost object.[25]*

If a doctor has to ask for permission to perform an autopsy, he should remember that the bereaved person will probably be in the state described above, and consenting could feel to him like agreeing to the cutting up of a living person.

The pangs of grief gradually give way to depression and despair as the person unlearns the habits he has woven around the relationship with the deceased. The waves of grief lessen in frequency and intensity. Commonly a watershed occurs after about two years. Appetite and pride in appearance return and a new life is constructed. The process of adjustment is easier for the elderly who expect death to come to their dearest, but for the young widow or parent it is harder.

Good general advice for the bereaved, particularly in countries whose traditions derive from Britain, is "don't try to be too wonderful. Let other people help you."

To be able to counsel the bereaved effectively, the counsellor

* Dr. Bowlby is not being callous in referring to someone a person loves as an "object"—it is an expression used regularly by psychologists.

himself needs to see death as a meaningful event. He must talk
frankly with grieving people, both during the period before the
death and afterwards. In his book *Bereavement* (see Bibliography)
Dr. Colin Murray Parkes points out that

> "pain is inevitable in such a case and cannot be avoided. It stems
> from the awareness of both parties that neither can give the
> other what he wants. The helper cannot bring back the person
> who is dead and the bereaved person cannot gratify the helper
> by seeming helped. No wonder that both feel dissatisfied with
> the encounter."

During the period of numbness and also during the early phase
of the acute pangs of grief, bereaved people need help with almost
everything, and especially with decisions. They need mothering.
Hence the Jewish custom for the whole family to rally round the
household during the period of "Shiva" (seven days). Running the
house and the funeral is not the duty of the dead person's nearest
and dearest : they need very practical help; sympathy can come
later, in the form of tolerance of the depression and irritability
which may afflict the bereaved for several months.

The helpers should do nothing which will discourage the
expression of appropriate grief. They should make it clear to the
grieving person that they do not mind if he weeps. Over the next
few weeks visits from friends will be appreciated, even if they are
awkward occasions. The friends may find that they have to share
some of the pain, to reassure the grieving person that his disorgan-
ization is normal and not a sign that he is going mad. Any mention
of suicide, however, should be taken seriously and is an indication
for referral to a psychiatrist for help.

In a hospice there are often a number of bereaved people who
are working through their grief by doing voluntary work for a few
months following the death. The best help for the grieving, however,
comes from other people who are in the same situation. Bereaved
mothers or widows are more likely to find support from other
parents or widows similarly stricken than they are within their
own families.[48] A local clergyman can often bring together a group
of widows for self-help, and there are two organizations which are
rapidly becoming nationally important in this field. "Cruse,"*

* Head Office: The Charter House, 6 Lion Gate Gardens, Richmond,
Surrey. (01-940 2660.)

founded in 1959 by Margaret Torrie, gives practical and friendly advice and help to widows and their children, by the provision of information sheets and by direct counselling on a local or national level.

Though Cruse clubs are social clubs in several parts of the country, the main function of the national organization is not to provide social support but a counselling service to widows, particularly those in the younger age group. They need friends badly, because the widow is often a social misfit who does not get invited out. This social isolation should be broken, especially at Christmas, and in the case of young widows, with baby-sitting help. Only 6% of women who are widowed between twenty and fifty years of age will eventually remarry. They are a potentially very lonely group.[137] If grief is further complicated by financial hardship due to the death of the breadwinner, considerable support will be needed from social workers, health visitors, child guidance officers, housing departments and many others.[201]

The other organization similar to Cruse, which helps the parents of dead or chronically ill children is the Society of Compassionate Friends,* founded in 1969 by Rev. Simon Stephens. Such magnificent institutions as these are long overdue, and more help is still needed for the older age groups of widows and widowers. They help people over some of the most painful experiences of life. For bereavement can feel like mutilation. Similar patterns of grieving are indeed experienced by people who have lost a limb or a home.[162] The person's whole balance of health is disturbed. During the first six months of bereavement the death rate among widowers in one study was 40% higher than expected. They died mainly from coronary thromboses—broken hearts in every sense.[160] Widows have more trouble from their arthritis, asthma and ulcerative colitis than do their married counterparts,[123] requiring double the number of medical consultations for their osteo-arthritis.[49] It has even been suggested that grief can occasionally cause or precipitate cancer, especially in people with personalities which do not respond aggressively to stress.[118]

A wide variety of psychiatric illnesses may also be precipitated by a bereavement though it is possible that the person had them in a mild form before the stress of grief was added.[158] Dr. George

* Head Office: 8 Westfield Road, Rugby, Warwickshire. (Tel: 0788-5087.)

Engel found that actual pain may be experienced, sometimes mimicking that of the deceased person.[61]

One particularly difficult day is the first anniversary of the death. A visit from a friend, clergyman or doctor is then welcomed, and some hospices send a postcard with an offer of help if needed.

After two years or so, it may eventually be appropriate to point out to a person who is still grieving that their duty to the dead is now done and grieving has gone on long enough. A memorial service or a visit to the grave may help with making the break. It is now time to turn out to other people again; to redecorate the house.

Pathological Grief

"The bereaved searches the time before the death for evidence of failure to do right by the lost one. He accuses himself of negligence and exaggerates minor omissions. After the fire disaster the central topic of discussion for a young married woman was the fact that her husband died after he left her following a quarrel, and of a young man whose wife died that he fainted too soon to save her.

"By appropriate techniques these distorted pictures can be successfully transformed into a normal grief reaction with resolution."[123]—Dr. Erich Lindemann

This transformation is effected mainly by someone who is prepared to listen without criticism to the bitterness and guilt which the bereaved person pours out. He finds that it is safe to let out these bottled-up feelings, and is free to get on with his "grief work."

Grieving people are more likely to need the help of a psychiatrist than they were before the bereavement.[158] Women, particularly younger ones, are thought to be more prone to this than men, at least in the first year. A number of situations may alert one to a danger of psychiatric disturbance with abnormally long or intense grieving. For instance, if there is obvious animosity between the dying person and the survivor, then the latter is apt to suffer afterwards from feelings of anger or guilt. People who have very intense pining or who have grief-prone personalities that have reacted badly to loss in the past, especially need to be befriended. So do those who are socially isolated or in whom the phase of depression leads to a withdrawn or "living in the past" attitude. They, and people who feel guilty for stopping their mourning, are liable to sink into a state of perpetual grief which robs them of joy for life. This is a particular risk with the elderly, and might possibly be averted by regular visits from a health visitor who could also ensure that they eat an adequate diet.[10, 245]

The normal process of unlearning the urge to recover the dead person can be impeded if an abnormal stimulus to the memory is encountered, leading to chronic grief. For this reason widows should be discouraged from attending spiritualist seances and the like. Even if some part of the dead man's personality is being contacted, it cannot be a part of any importance, since the "messages" passed on are such inconsequential rubbish.[18]

Dickens furnished us with a splendid description of chronic grief in *The Old Curiosity Shop*, though it is often more painful than this :

> ". . . she told her how she had wept and moaned and prayed to die herself, when this had happened; and how when she first came to that place (the graveside of her husband), a young creature strong in love and grief, she had hoped that her heart was breaking as it seemed to be. But that time passed by, and although she continued to be sad when she came there, still she could bear to come, and so went on until it was pain no longer, but a solemn pleasure, and a duty she had learned to like. And now that five-and-fifty years were gone, she spoke of the dead man as if he had been her son or grandson, with a kind of pity for his youth. . . ."

In this state a widow may be hallucinated with visions of the dead, though simple illusions of his presence are more common. She conceives her duty to be towards the man who has gone rather than towards the all-too-pressing needs of those still living.

Another kind of bereavement which often causes trouble is the death of a child. "Cot deaths," accidents or teenage suicides are particularly traumatic for the parents, who may feel guilty and desperate, sometimes even committing suicide themselves. "Why was I not more careful or more understanding?" they ask. If no-one listens to this tirade of self-reproach, it may become a lifelong burden. If the marriage is already under strain, or if the dead child was an only child, the problem is even worse.[151]

The child found dead in his cot for no apparent reason is causing concern to modern paediatricians. To the distress of the family are added the humiliating implications of a coroner's investigation. When he decides it was a "cot death," the coroner will frequently refer the family to a paediatrician interested in the problem, who can reassure them and compare their case with other similar ones.[33, 59] An organization has just been founded in London to deal with these emergencies.* It has research and welfare departments.

Grieving Children

Grief in children is more likely to follow pathological patterns. There is some evidence that infants in particular tend to suppress grief, so that it manifests much later as an apparently unrelated symptom. The same reactions can be sparked off by temporary separation from the mother, observation of which has led to the present day concern over "maternal deprivation."[24, 26] The same problems can arise, however, in children separated from other familiar elements in their environment, and the whole topic is being currently reconsidered. The result, however, may perhaps be psychiatric or even criminal behaviour in later life.[201, 238] It was found, for instance, that one third of the women in Holloway Prison were fatherless.[35] If it is the father who dies, someone in the child's life may be needed to fill some of his functions, even if only seen infrequently. A psychiatrist, family doctor or priest may be able to be the source of advice, direction and discipline which is needed. One organization which comes near to replacing the father is the Australian institution "Legacy" which enabled servicemen who had survived the war to give long term support to the widows and children of their comrades who had died.

It is commonly supposed that if the death is hushed up and never mentioned, the child will not grieve, but this could not be further from the truth.[236] It may be noted that his school performance deteriorates, and that he manifests anxiety. Children aged between six and ten are apt to feel guilty about the death, and to wonder whether it was something that they did which caused it— an anxiety which can be easily relieved if detected. It is essential to

---

* Foundation for the Study of Infant Deaths, 23 St. Peter's Square, London W6 9NW. (01-748 7768.)

be frank with children, and to let them grieve with the parents, who need not be afraid to show distress or to talk about their sorrow.

Helping the Grief of the Dying

As I pointed out in Chapter 9 (p. 110), the dying man will be grieving as surely as his relatives. This will be hardest for the person who is leaving a successful well-integrated life with strong ties to people and possessions. As Dr. C. Knight Aldrich wrote : "Strength of personality may help a patient not so much to avoid depression in anticipation of death as to conceal the depression from others."[7] Perhaps the way to help in making this grief bearable is to enable the dying man to feel useful to other people. I have known many dying patients who taught students on ward rounds with great zest, telling them about pain control, why they no longer believed in euthanasia, and how they were being helped to face death themselves. On the cover of this book is a picture of a patient who urged me to include a chapter on religion. "It becomes so important to you : you must include it," he said, and Chapter 12 will indeed incorporate several of his suggestions.

A dying person can help his family to begin to anticipate what life will be like without him. If he has discussed with his wife her plans for the future and the provisions in his will, it will be much easier for her to adjust to her future as a widow. Just before he died, Hans Zinsser, an American bacteriologist, consoled his wife by writing sonnets for her. Here are some of his lines :[250]

> When I am gone—and I shall go before you—
> Think of me not as your disconsolate lover;
> Think of the joy it gave me to adore you,
> Of sun and stars you helped me to discover.
>
> And this still living part of me will come
> to sit beside you, in the empty room.
>
> Then all on Earth that Death has left behind
> Will be the merry part of me within your mind.

The Need for Mourning

Traditional patterns of living usually incorporate a means of formal expression of grief. There was the Victorian funeral, with its hearse and flowers and black crape; the prescribed oration of the Kaddish[78] in the Orthodox Synagogue service, to be spoken by a recently-bereaved Jew every week for eleven months and on the anniversary of the death; the pomp and dignity of state funerals; the old Irish keening wake in which women swayed all night in a trance-like state, chanting dirges.

Every culture has had its equivalent ceremony, but today in Britain this need is frequently unsatisfied. The bereaved are avoided, with their grief bottled up,[81] like a poison which, instead of being thrown out by the body, stays to damage it. Somehow we manage to ignore death. We rarely see anyone die; most of us have never seen a corpse; we seldom teach our medical students anything about it.[207, 243] In American funeral parlours cosmetics and smile-fixers are used on the corpse to reinforce this great denial.

The bereaved Jew and his family have clearly defined duties throughout the period of mourning, and each knows what is expected of him. In Victorian England the rituals of mourning were even more rigid, as these passages from Spon's Household Manual of 1894 show:

"A widow's mourning is the deepest, and continued longest. For the first twelve months the dress and mantle must be of paramatta, the skirt of the dress covered with crape, put on in one piece to within an inch of the waist; sleeves tight to the arm, bodice entirely covered with crape . . . and deep lawn collar. The mantle . . . is very heavily trimmed with crape. The widow's cap must be worn for a year, but not beyond the year."

"At the end of the sixth month (eighteen months in all) crape may be left off, and plain black worn for six months : and two years complete the period of mourning. For the first year, while a widow wears her weeds, she can, of course, accept no invitations; and it is in the worst possible taste for her to be seen in any place of public resort. After the first year she can, if so disposed, gradually resume her place in society."

Even the width of the black edging round a mourner's visiting card, and the depth of mourning appropriate for a second cousin were laid down meticulously. Grief was thus made external to the person, formalized and thus "detoxicated." Nowadays we often do not even say farewells.

To counter this trend, hospices nearly all have a "viewing chapel" where the body, not degraded by cosmetics or other attempts to conceal what it is, is decently laid for the family, if they wish, to take their leave. Prayers can be repeated if required, without disturbing patients in the ward. Children of the family should be admitted also so that someone can explain that Grandad has gone, and left his body behind.

The English like to grieve in staunch silence, but this is not a universal behaviour pattern, and people should be allowed to grieve in their own way. I can remember a horrified nun in St. Joseph's Hospice who recounted how seventeen members of an old Italian grandfather's family gradually gathered round his bed during his last night. They waited tense and poised as his breathing failed. Sister knelt beside him, repeated the prayers for the dying and felt his pulse. It flickered to a stop and she said "He's gone now," whereupon the entire company burst out howling and two disconsolate women hurled themselves whooping across his chest in paroxysms of remorse. The corpse took a mighty gasping breath and uttered a final satisfied groan.

There is an old Irish charm against sorrow, which was translated by Lady Gregory as follows :

The charm which God set for Himself when the divinity within Him was darkened.

A charm to be said by the cross when the night is black and the soul is heavy with sorrow.

A charm to be said at sunrise, with the hands on the breast, when the eyes are red with weeping, and the madness of grief is strong.

A charm that has no words :—only the silent prayer.

Kalorama: St. Joannes de Deo Verpleeghuis, Nijmegen, Holland

12

The Role of Religion

THE greatest pain of all, which I mentioned in Chapter 9, comes from a great inner longing. This feeling of lack, or inadequacy, or sin, or however it expresses itself, can only be ministered to from one of the great religious teachings.[248] We have built ourselves a fortress of personality in which to hide and have thought of ourselves as only a body which we feed, pamper, adorn and display with all our energy. When the body is spoiled and the fortress crumbles, we are compelled to search for something more permanent than either. Mr. R., the old Glaswegian convict whose story I told earlier, said to me one day, after a little reflection, "Recently I've thought about religion, because I'm nearing death."

Which Religion?

There are many practical points in the care of patients who are adherents of different faiths.

Roman Catholics have merged Extreme Unction with the Anointing of the Sick which can if appropriate lead into Communion, Confession and Absolution. This wise arrangement will give great comfort to the relatives, without unduly frightening the patient. It is desirable that a priest be present with a dying Catholic.

If none is available, then anyone may encourage the patient to ask forgiveness for sins. And incidentally, cremation is permissible for Catholics nowadays. The Anglican approach is broadly similar, but is less likely to be so formalized unless the patient requests the sacraments. Having no ritual framework, the Nonconformist minister is thrown back on his own wisdom, resource and goodness. All may use the reading of scripture.[187]

Rabbis will also wish to read a confessional service, acknowledging the need for spiritual healing. In the case of an Orthodox Jew, the body may be removed to the mortuary, with the arms and hands extended at the sides of the body,[122] but cleansing will be carried out by members of a special Burial Society.[78] Dissection or removal of any organs except the cornea is avoided. Preferably the body should not be left unattended until the funeral. Burial follows, and should be as soon as possible. Liberal Jews relax most of these rules.

Moslems have even stricter rules :[3, 17] the Minister will usually tell the patient that he will soon die, and urge him to confess sins and beg forgiveness. If at all possible, the family should be present when he dies, and thereafter they must wash and prepare the body. It will be left facing Mecca and only relatives or friends should move it. No infidel should touch the body on any account, and a post mortem must be avoided at all costs. Not even the cornea may be removed. Moslems are always buried, with no coffin.

In order to enter his next life in a good state, the Buddhist needs, above all, to die happy. When the patient is found to have a terminal illness, a Buddhist monk from the nearest Vihara should be asked to befriend him. At the appropriate time he will want to recite Sutras and bless the patient, asking him to recall his *good* deeds. A monk with a picture of the Buddha will try to be present at the moment of death, but afterwards all funeral services are considered as grief therapy for the relatives.

Hindus have a more exacting ritual. The priest may tie a thread round the neck or wrist of the patient to signify a blessing. The thread should not be removed. Immediately after death he will pour water into the mouth of the body, while the family wash it. As many Hindus are particular about who should touch the body, one should ask first. They will require a cremation as soon as possible.

While the various observances of different religions are almost quaint in their differences, it is what they have in common that is most impressive. All religions demand that those ministering to the dying shall preserve as peaceful an atmosphere as possible for the patient. Afterwards, they all agree that the body must be treated with respect and gentleness. The reason for this latter is generally forgotten, but a Moslem will insist that although the connection between mind and body is broken at death, the actual separation takes much longer, and any carelessness in handling the corpse is felt as keenly by the patient as if he were alive.

Further, all the religions require that a dying man should go humbly, even apologetically, regretting folly but at the same time confident and rejoicing in divine Mercy. A man *in extremis* knows that he cannot get away with anything, that God is not mocked. If he knows about Justice (and in Britain everyone does) he may reasonably be terrified. The only consolation he could possibly be given in the light of this knowledge is to be reminded that Justice is only an aspect of Mercy, that this is the first quality radiated by the Godhead, and that it is boundless, without measure.

However, while this is fine for those who have a formalized faith, most of us are only vaguely Christian. To such, religion can be a help, perhaps proving at last a gateway to the inner treasure house. For such people religion must be always available, but never force-fed. Daily prayers in terminal wards are universally appreciated. Though some people do not take part, I have never heard anyone object. When a "nominal C of E" patient dies, an obvious need can be filled by familiar, non-sectarian prayers, and the joyful comfort of the twenty-third psalm. The chaplain (or the local vicar[74] if the patient is at home) should therefore introduce himself at least socially to every patient.

The Natural Religion

The chaplain of one hospice said that people who had not given a thought to religion, and those with a very strong religion, died more peacefully than those with a lukewarm faith whose ill-considered assumptions collapsed under stress. This observation was confirmed statistically by Professor Hinton.[93] But the most interesting group, the chaplain continued, were the three or four firm atheists whom he had seen die. Without exception they became enraged, and died in turmoil.

Because of his special training, a clergyman should always be called.[22, 130, 185] He will try to show the patient that "While I thought I was learning how to live, I was learning how to die," as Leonardo da Vinci expressed it. He will help him "to eliminate from his life—his actual present earthly life—all the elements of destruction, and of decay, corruption, bitterness, resentment and hatred : all those things which kill a soul."[23] Of course if no priest is available, or if the patient cannot accept one, there is no reason why other members of the caring team should not give this help.[104] The message may be, "I don't know why this is happening; but I know it will be *all right*."[64, 146]

All that I have said in previous chapters about counselling—of both the dying and the bereaved—could be the function of the clergyman, who is often the member of the team most suited to the task.[13] It is a matter of uncovering hidden inner knowledge.

So much for people with a formal religion. But we are now seeing increasing numbers of people who can believe in nothing but the body and personality. For a Christian to try to communicate in these circumstances can be like trying to talk to an uncomprehending foreigner. It can be disconcerting when all one's beliefs and terminology are questioned.

The Romans met this problem when they established law courts in new colonies. Some of the disputes arising knew no precedent in Roman Law. So they fell back on the traditional laws of the colonists, the Jus Gentium. But if there was no guide there either, the judge would appeal to Jus Naturale : the natural justice self-evident to all men.

There is a parallel here. If a man has a religion, we must respect and obey it. But if he has none, we have to fall back on the Natural Religion, because his needs are still the same. That is to say that you have to answer the patient's questions, or face his fears, quite naked of comfortably formalized ideas. You have to speak the Truth as you know it at the time, fresh and alive; precisely appropriate to this man and his present needs.

The Douglas Macmillan Home, Stoke-on-Trent

13

What is Death?

IF we would care for the dying we must first bring order to our own philosophy about death. Caring for a man in trouble means facing trouble with him. If we cannot face it, we will fail him. But having a philosophy does not mean having all the answers. It means holding to principles, and being content to fill in the details later should they ever be needed.

What happens?

The only natural cause of death is old age, but it is uncommon to die of this, and to judge by his statistical reports, the Registrar General doesn't believe in it at all! (see p. 86 and Figure B, p. 80). Most of us die of disease of some kind, unless we meet death suddenly in an accident. When the death is not sudden, it is evident that it proceeds in distinct stages. Even physical death advances by degrees. Organs fail at different rates, and when the body begins to die it does so from below upwards. Use of the legs is lost before that of the arms, the abdominal organs cease to function before those in the chest, the feet are cold before the head.

A man's mind may be intact until the body dies, or it may disintegrate first, sometimes very gradually. The death of the personality can appear like death of the man himself if we have never looked at the person more deeply than to see his social machinery. Like the body, however, the personality is just a bag of tools. The blunting of these instruments has rarely been so well described as in a Personal Paper in the Lancet some years ago.[167]

This mind is not dependent on the body for its life. If the mind is disturbed enough, the body will die, as the practice of voodoo magic has shown. Harvey Cox wrote :

"Anthropologists who investigate magical beliefs among tribal peoples today report that violating a taboo can cause death, and that people who have been killed in effigy by voodoo techniques do in fact die with more than accidental frequency. The reason for this is that a personality system includes organic, social and cultural components. A person whose whole view of himself includes the cultural meanings inherent in a magical society will literally die if that culture indicates he should. Culture has a powerful effect on persons, far more than we were willing to admit during the eighteenth and nineteenth centuries, when rationalistic individualism laughed at such things."[39]

A scientific look at people with a predilection to death has shown that such forces also operate in our own society, if more hidden.[235]

To tell us what happens at death, who better than someone who has encountered it. A friend of mine was drowned, but resuscitated, so I asked him to write down what he experienced. Here is his account :

"When I was seven years old, I used to go to a boating pond in the local park; for six pennies, I could take out a boat for half an hour.

"On one occasion, my boat got stuck at the side of the bank, and in attempting to push myself free, I overturned the boat and fell into the water. The water was not very deep, but I was fully submerged until I was pulled free by somebody, probably the park-keeper. I do not know how long I stayed below the surface of the pond, it could have been less than a minute. However, I shall describe the episode *as I experienced it*, and not as it 'must' or 'should' have been.

"I recall an element of surprise, but no panic or fear. Nor did I feel any physical pain or suffering of any kind. Nevertheless, I had a sense that death was near. At some point, I became aware of my whole body as being separate from me, and this awareness extended to include children playing in a nearby shallow pond. I was aware of trees surrounding the pond, the covering sky, groups of people and a woman walking along pushing a pram. This awareness was extended as much underwater as above it: in particular, a small fish swam into view. I became acutely conscious that the feeling of my own being included that of this creature; in fact, there were not two separate beings, only one, although the *body* of the fish and *my* body were separate. This *knowledge* communicated itself *mutually*, as a felt experience.

"Throughout this period, I was making no effort to save myself. I felt embraced by a Great Presence in which I experienced utter peace; a pure, still joy to which the normal experiences of pleasure or happiness bear no relation, and yet I cannot remember anything so thrilling; and the certainty of absolute invulnerability—nothing, but nothing, could as much as scratch what I am. This Presence was, although possessing no form, *not* impersonal: the inclination is to say He, rather than It. I was fully known by this Presence which had enveloped me with such love and care.

"Whilst in this state, I experienced visually my entire childhood; imagine a film of seven years' duration seen in the 'twinkling of an eye'! Yet it was more than visual, for I was left with a 'taste,' a kind of distilled quality or essence of those years. This was just observed—I do not recall any value-judgement about it.

"On a few occasions since this experience, I have known that sense of complete invulnerability, already referred to. It has arisen in moments of actual or possible danger."

Death is a Mystery

To die is different from what anyone supposed—and luckier.
—Walt Whitman.

By the Law of England a man is dead when two doctors, with no professional or other interest in his death, have pronounced him dead. The Bar Council has firmly declined to define death more precisely than that, and as far as I know, no one else has ever done better. (Recent experience in intensive care units, for instance, has shown that the electro-encephalogram is at best only an indicator, with no absolute authority). The fact that such difficulty is encountered in defining death suggests that we are dealing with something mysterious. The modern mind dislikes mysteries. Even our architecture banishes dark corners: everything has to be flat and open. But death *is* a mystery.

On one of the few occasions when I heard a patient ask "Am I dying?" the doctor's reply was "No. But your body soon will." In this form, the message was acceptable, and did not give rise to despair or fear. Only when we give the name "I" to something which is not "I" can death be fearful.

> "Birth forces the baby out of the protective seclusion of the womb into the human family: death forces the same individual out of a now familiar society into the unknown, leaving behind a physical body to disintegrate in a tomb and some sort of a gap in that society, which others in their turn will fill. . . . It is entirely natural and understandable that we should feel afraid of death, for it mutilates body and mind, which together form our image of ourselves as 'us,' it forces us to leave those near and dear to us and the familiar world around us, and to give up our hold on life as we know it."[236]

An eddy in a turbulent river has its own sound and its own form, and its special relationship with other swirling eddies, then it rejoins the great river. Perhaps it grieves! The traditional answer to such mysteries—that when you die you go to heaven, as John Smith, recognizable and still separate, possibly with a purgatorial wait first—does not satisfy many people nowadays. Where such simple faith survives it is beautiful, appropriate and deeply to be respected, but the idea no longer rings true to most people.[64]

This is no cause for sadness, since the idea was at best an attempt to express the inexpressible. It never could be more than an allegory. We should therefore look to see what truth it was trying to portray, and how this can be reinterpreted to people of today.

So, What is Death?

To care for the dying is a very human occupation which offers an opportunity for pure giving, because the dying man can never repay what he receives.

At the hour of our death the great need is for stillness, and that is available in abundance. Peace I leave with you, my peace I give unto you: not as the world giveth give I unto you. Let not your heart be troubled, neither let it be afraid.—*John* 14.27.

In the moment of death, something departs, leaving the body behind. It is the moment when a man leaves his body. Death is therefore a change of form. It is widely believed that a soul survives, in some other form. In the East it has always been held that the soul returns to manifest again in a new body.

Plato also deduced this, as he recounted in Book Ten of *The Republic* :

> The daughter of Necessity is speaking to the dead : "Souls of a day, a new generation of men shall here begin the cycle of its mortal existence. Your destiny shall not be allotted to you : you shall choose it freely for yourselves. Let him who draws the first lot be the first to choose his next life which shall be his irrevocably. But virtue owns no master : as a man honours or slights her, so he shall have more of her or less. The responsibility lies with the chooser : Heaven is blameless.". . . "it was a truly amazing sight to watch how each soul selected its life—a sight at once sad, and ludicrous, and strange, for the choice was largely governed by the habits of their previous life."

Plato's scheme certainly has its appeal, since it displays absolute Justice, yet permits of unimpeded improvement by postulating a dimension beyond time.

Whatever one believes, all great teachers have accepted that the dying man must prepare for another world. Never should this preparation be interfered with. It is helped by simple qualities such as goodness and beauty, with which we should surround the dying. The traditional symbols and ceremonies of our religions provide for this need. At death a man's mental possessions all fall away, so that when he really is dying he should be given only the Truth, not what we suppose might please him—there is nothing left which can be pleased or displeased.

And I repeat, he needs us to be still.

So : What is Death?

References

1 Adams, G. F., "Personal View," *B.M.J.*, 1969, vol. 4, p. 363.
2 Agate, J., *The Practice of Geriatrics* (Heinemann, 1970, p. 180).
3 Ahmed, K. S., "Taking Medicines During Ramadan," *B.M.J.*, 1971, vol. 4, p. 425.
4 Aitken-Swan, J., "Nursing the Late Cancer Patient at Home," *Practitioner*, 1959, vol. 183, p. 64.
5 Aitken-Swan, J. and Easson, E. C., "Reactions of Cancer Patients on Being Told Their Diagnosis," *B.M.J.*, 1959, vol. 1, p. 779.
6 Alderson, M. R., "Care of the Dying," *B.M.J.*, 1973, vol. 1, p. 170.
7 Aldrich, C. K., "The Dying Patient's Grief," *Journal of the American Medical Association*, 1963, vol. 184, no. 5, p. 329.
8 Alvarez, W. C., "Care of the Dying," *Journal of the American Medical Association*, 1952, vol. 150, p. 86.
9 Amulree, Lord, "15th James MacKenzie Lecture," *Journal of the Royal College of General Practitioners*, 1969, vol. 17, p. 3.
10 Anderson, W. F., "A Death in the Family," *B.M.J.*, 1973, vol. 1, p. 31.
11 Anon. "The Importance of Death," *World Medicine*, August, 1968.
12 Anon. "Death in the First Person," *American Journal of Nursing*, February, 1970, p. 335.
13 Autton, N., *Christian Pastoral Care of the Bereaved* (symposium, January, 1970, by Institute of Religion and Medicine, 58A Wimpole Street, London W.1).
14 Bacon, F., "Of Death," *Essaies of Sr. Francis Bacon* (John Beale, London, 1612).
15 Bailey, M., "A Survey of the Social Needs of Patients with Incurable Lung Cancer," *Almoner*, 1959, vol. 11, p. 379.
16 Banks, A. L., "Euthanasia," *Practitioner*, 1948, vol. 161, p. 101.
17 Baqui, A. (Mufti), *Muslim Teaching Concerning Death* (A St. Joseph's Hospice Occasional Paper. St. Joseph's Hospice, Mare Street, London E.8).
18 Barber, H., "The Act of Dying," *Practitioner*, 1948, vol. 161, p. 76.
19 Barnes, D., *Enduring to the End* (Letters to the Editor, *The Times*, 22nd April, 1970).
20 Beeches, H. K., "The Screaming Wounded Soldier Didn't Need Any Sort of Overdose," *Hospital Times*, 6th February, 1970.
21 Bentley, G. B., *Decisions About Life and Death* (Church Information Office, Dean's Yard, London S.W.1).

146

References

22 Birley, M. F., "Terminal Care," *Almoner*, 1960, vol. 13, p. 86.
23 Bloom, A. (Metropolitan Anthony), *Speech*, summarized in Newsletter No. 20 (April, 1972) of Institute of Religion and Medicine (see Ref. 13).
24 Bowlby, J., "Grief and Mourning in Infancy and Early Childhood," *Psychoanalytic Study of the Child*, 1960, vol. 15, p. 9.
25 Bowlby, J., "Processes of Mourning" *International Journal of Psychoanalyisis*, 1961, vol. 42, p. 317.
26 Bowlby, J., "Pathological Mourning and Childhood Mourning," *Journal of the American Psychoanalysis Association*, 1963, vol. 11, p. 500.
27 *British Journal of Geriatric Practice*, "An Alternative to Euthanasia," March 1969, p. 5.
28 British Medical Association, *The Problem of Euthanasia* (Booklet from B.M.A., Tavistock Square, London W.C.1).
29 *British Medical Journal*, "Termination of Life," 1971, vol. 1, p. 187.
30 *Ditto*, "Treatment of Carcinoma of the Larynx," 1971, vol. 1, p. 417.
31 *Ditto*, "Operating on the Elderly," 1972, vol. 2, p. 489.
32 *Ditto*, "Tragic Dilemma," 1972, vol. 4, p. 567.
33 *Ditto*, "Unexpected Deaths of Babies," 1973, vol. 1, p. 308.
34 Brocklehurst, J. C., "Co-ordination in the Care of the Elderly," *Lancet*, 1966, vol. 1, p. 1363.
35 Brown F., *Bereaved Children* (same source as ref. 13).
36 Cade, S., *Cancer: the Patient's Viewpoint and the Clinician's Problems* (Proceedings of Royal Society of Medicine, 1963, vol. 56, p. 1).
37 Caldwell, J. R., "The Management of Inoperable Malignant Disease in General Practice," *Journal of the College of General Practitioners*, 1964, vol. 8, p. 23.
38 Colebrook, L., "Euthanasia," *Lancet*, 1961, vol. 2, p. 485.
39 Cox, H., *The Church in the Secular City* (Pelican, 1968), p. 162.
40 Cramond, W. A., "Psychotherapy of the Dying Patient," *B.M.J.*, 1970, vol. 3, p. 389.
41 Cronk, H. M., "This Business of Dying," *Nursing Times*, 31st August, 1972.
42 Curran, C. "Is There a Right to Kill?" *Sunday Telegraph*, 30th March, 1969.
43 Cushing, H., *The Life of Sir William Osler* (Oxford University Press, 1940, vol. 2, p. 620).
44 *Daily Mail*, "Allow These Children to Die" (12th August, 1972).
45 *Daily Telegraph*, "Let Spina Bifidas Die" (12th August, 1972).
46 Daniel, M. P., "The Social Worker's Role," *B.M.J.*, 1973, vol. 1, p. 36.
47 Daube, D., *Sanctity of Life* (Proceedings of Royal Society of Medicine, 1967, vol. 60, p. 1235).
48 Davis, J. A., "The Attitude of Parents to the Approaching Death of Their Child," *Developmental Medicine and Child Neurology*, 1964, vol. 6, p. 286.

49 Deutch, H., "Absence of Grief," *Psychoanalysis Quarterly*, 1937, vol. 6, p. 12.

50 Donaldson, M., "Cancer, the Psychological Disease," *Lancet*, 1955, vol. 1, p. 959.

51 Dott, N. M., *Discussion on the Treatment of Intractable Pain* (Proceedings of Royal Society of Medicine, 1959, vol. 52, p. 987).

52 Downie, P. A., "The Physiotherapist and the Patient with Cancer," *Physiotherapy*, March, 1971, p. 117.

53. Downie, P. A., "Rehabilitation Following Mastectomy," *Nursing Mirror*, 15th September, 1972.

54 Downie, P. A., "Paraplegia, Amputations and Head and Neck Surgery," *Nursing Mirror*, 22nd September, 1972.

55 Downie, P. A., "Persistent Cancer," *Nursing Mirror*, 29th September, 1972.

56 Downing, A. B., *Euthanasia and Christianity* (Reprint from Modern Free Churchman, from Voluntary Euthanasia Society, 13 Prince of Wales Terrace, London, W.8).

57 Earengay, W. G., "Voluntary Euthanasia," *Medico-Legal Criminology Review*, 1940, vol. 8, p. 91.

58 Ellison-Nash, D. F., *The impact of total care, with special reference to Myelodysplasia.* Developmental Medicine and Child Neurology, Supplement 22, 1970, p. 1.

59 Emery, J. L., "Welfare of Families of Children Found Unexpectedly Dead," *B.M.J.*, 1972, vol. 1, p. 612.

60 Emrys-Roberts, R. M., "Death and Resuscitation," *B.M.J.*, 1969, vol. 4, p. 364.

61 Engel, G. L., "Psychogenic Pain and the Pain-Prone Patient," *American Journal of Medicine*, 1959, vol. 26, p. 899.

62 Epictetus, *Dissertations* I, IX, 16.

63 Exton-Smith, A. N., "Terminal Illness in the Aged," *Lancet*, 1961, vol. 2, p. 305.

64 Fawell, R. M., *Death is a Horizon* (Friends' House, London, N.W.1).

65 Finlay, H. V. L., "Selecting Cases of Myelomeningocele for Surgery," *B.M.J.*, 1971, vol. 3, p. 429.

66 Flood, P., *Morals and Medicine* (Catholic Truth Society, 201 Victoria Street, London S.W.1).

67 Fox, T. F., "The Greater Medical Profession," *Lancet*, 1956, vol. 2, p. 779.

68 Fox, T. F., "Purposes of Medicine," *Lancet*, 1965, vol. 2, p. 801.

69 French, D. G., "The Care of Cancer in Practice," *Practitioner*, 1956, vol. 177, p. 78.

70 Gardham, J., *Palliative Surgery* (Royal Society of Medicine, 1964, vol. 57, p. 123).

71 Gavey, C. J., *Discussion on Palliation in Cancer* (Proceedings of Royal Society of Medicine, 1955, vol. 48, p. 703).

72 Geriscope, *Geriatrics*, May 1971, p. 26.

73 Gerle, B., Lunden, G., and Sandblom, P., "The Patient with Inoper-

able Cancer from the Psychiatric and Social Standpoints," *Cancer,* 1960, vol. 13, p. 1206.

74 Gibson, R., "Ethics and Management of Advanced Cancer," *B.M.J.,* 1962, vol. 2, p. 977.

75 Gibson, R. "Supporting the Patient in the Home," *B.M.J.* 1973, vol. 1, p. 35.

76 Giles, L., *Musings of a Chinese Mystic* (Murray, London, 1955), p. 32.

77 Gillon, R., "Voluntary Euthanasia," *Oxford Medical School Gazette,* 1964, vol. 16, p. 49.

78 Goldberg, P. S., *Jewish Mourning Rituals* (Same source as ref. 13).

79 Gould, D., "A Better Way to Die," *New Statesman,* 4th April, 1969.

80 Graeme, P., "St. Luke's" *St. Mary's Hospital Gazette,* 1966, vol. 4.

81 Greer, G., "Not A Time to Die," *Sunday Times,* 3rd December, 1972.

82 *Guy's Gazette,* "The Happy Release" (14th March, 1970).

83 *Hackney Gazette,* "Introducing St. Joseph's Hospice" (30th June, 1972).

84 Hancock, S., "A Death in the Family," *B.M.J.,* 1973, vol. 1, p. 29.

85 *Hansard,* House of Lords (1st December, 1936, vol. 103, pp. 465–506).

6 *Hansard,* House of Lords (28th November, 1959, vol. 169, pp. 552–598).

87 *Hansard,* House of Lords (25th March, 1969, vol. 300, pp. 1143–1254).

88 *Hansard,* House of Commons (7th April, 1970, vol. 799, pp. 252–258).

89 Hart, F. D., Taylor, R. T. and Huskisson, E. C., "Pain at Night," *Lancet,* 1970, vol. 1, p. 881.

90 Haskard, O., "Slippery Slope" (29th March, 1969, Letter to *The Times*).

91 Heenan, J., "The Need for Plain Speaking" (26th March, 1969, Letter to *The Times*).

92 Henke, E., *Unpublished essay by a patient* (St. Christopher's Hospice, Lawrie Park Road, London, S.E.26).

93 Hinton, J. M., "The Physical and Mental Distress of the Dying," *Quarterly Journal of Medicine,* 1963, vol. 32, p.1.

94 Hinton, J. M., "Facing Death," *Journal of Psychosomatic Research,* 1966, vol. 10, p. 22.

95 Holford, J., "Terminal Care," *Nursing Times* booklet, 1973.

96 Howell, D. A., "A Child Dies," *Journal of Pediatric Surgery,* 1966, vol. 1, p. 2.

97 Hughes, H. L. G., *Peace at the Last* (Calouste Gulbenkian Foundation, London, 1960).

98 Human Rights Society, *Licensed to Kill?* (from 27 Walpole Street, London, S.W.3.)

99 Irvine, R. E., "Progressive Patient Care in the Geriatric Unit," *Postgraduate Medical Journal,* 1963, vol. 39, p. 401.

100 Irvine, R. E., "The Day Hospital in Geriatrics," *Update,* 1969, vol. 1, p. 329.

101 Irvine, R. E., and Smith, B. J., "Patterns of Visiting," *Lancet*, 1963, vol. 1, p. 597.

102 Jackson, D., *Euthanasia—A Christian Viewpoint* (Pacemaker, April-June 1971. *Nurses' Christian Fellowship Magazine.*)

103 Joseph, B., *Jewish Teaching Concerning Death* (St. Joseph's Hospice, see Ref. 17).

104 Kasley, V., "As Life Ebbs," *American Journal of Nursing*, vol. 48, no. 3, p. 170.

105 Kastenbaum, R., "Death and Responsibility," *Psychiatric Opinion*, 1966, vol. 3, pp. 5, 35.

106 Kay, W. W., "The Right to Die" (Letter to *The Times*, 1st May, 1970).

107 Kelly, W. D. and Friesen, S. R., "Do Cancer Patients Want to be Told?" *Surgery*, 1950, vol. 27, p. 822.

108 Kentish Times, *What's "Different" About St. Christopher's?* (Sidcup, 8th September, 1972).

109 Kubik, M. M., and Das Gupta, P. K., "Survival After 195 Defibrillations," *B.M.J.*, 1969, vol. 4, p. 432.

110 Lamerton, R., "Religion and the Care of the Dying," *Nursing Times*, 18th January, 1973.

111 Lamp Society, *Euthanasia—A Warning* (from 125 Heath Road, Bebington, Cheshire).

112 *Lancet*, "Euthanasia" (1961, vol. 2, p. 351).

113 Ditto "Prolongation of Dying" (1962, vol. 2, p. 1205).

114 Ditto "Care of the Dying" (1965, vol. 1, p. 424).

115 Ditto "The Blocked Bed" (1972, vol. 2, p. 221).

116 Ditto "Limitations of Resuscitation" (1972, vol. 1, p. 1169).

117 Lee, J., "The Nurse's Dilemma" (Letter to *Nursing Times*, 10th June, 1971).

118 Le Shan, L. L., "Psychological States as Factors in the Development of Malignant Disease," *Journal of the National Cancer Institute*, 1959, vol. 22, no. 1, p.1.

119 Le Shan, L. L., "The World of the Patient in Severe Pain of Long Duration," *Journal of Chronic Diseases*, 1964, vol. 17, p. 119.

120 Le Shan, L. L., *An Emotional Life-History Pattern Associated with Neoplastic Disease* (New York Academy of Sciences, 1966, vol. 125, no. 3, p. 780).

121 Le Shan, L. L. and Gassmann, M. L., "Some Observations on Psychotherapy with Patients Suffering from Neoplastic Diseases," *American Journal of Psychotherapy*, 1958, vol. 12, no. 4, p. 723.

122 Levenstein, M., *Jewish Teaching Concerning Death* (Same ref. as 103).

123 Lindemann, E., "Symptomatology and Management of Acute Grief," *American Journal of Psychiatry*, 1944, vol. 101, p. 141.

124 Lloyd-Roberts, G. C., "Developments in Orthopaedic Surgery in Childhood," *Nursing Mirror*, 8th August, 1972.

125 Lorber, J., "Results of Treatment of Myelomeningocele," *Developmental Medicine and Child Neurology*, 1971, vol. 13, p. 279.

126 Love, McN., "Management of Advanced Cancer," *B.M.J.*, 1962, vol. 2, p. 1192.
127 Macaulay, Lord, *History of England 1849*, vol. 1, p. 437.
128 MacMillan, S., "Margaret—A Study in Perception," *Nursing Times*, 28th December, 1972.
129 Marie Curie Memorial Foundation. *Some Simple Facts About Cancer* (pamphlet from 124 Sloane Street, London S.W.1).
130 Marie Curie Memorial Foundation. *Joint National Cancer Survey*, with the Queen's Institute of District Nursing: Report, 1952.
131 Matt. 19: v. 17–18; Exodus 20: v. 13; Buddhaghosa—Papancasudani: Sutta 9, "The Five Precepts of the Buddha".
132 Matthews, W. R., *Euthanasia and the Right to Death* (Voluntary Euthanasia Society: see Ref. 92).
133 McNulty, B. J., "The Needs of the Dying" (St. Christopher's Hospice: see Ref. 92).
134 McNulty, B. J., "Discharge of the Terminally-Ill Patient," *Nursing Times*, 10th September, 1970.
135 McNulty, B. J., *Care of the Dying* (copies of paper from St. Christopher's Hospice: Ref. 92).
136 McNulty, B. J., "Continuity of Care," *B.M.J.*, 1973, vol. 1, p. 38.
137 Melinski, M. A. H., *Widows in Society* (ref. 13).
138 Millard, C. K., "The Legalisation of Voluntary Euthanasia," *Public Health*, November, 1931.
139 Miller, M. B., "Decision-Making in the Death Process of the Ill Aged," *Geriatrics*, May, 1971.
140 Miller, E. J. and Gwynne, G. V., *Dependence, Independence and Counter-Dependence in Residential Institutions for Incurables* (Tavistock Institute of Human Relations, Belsize Lane, London N.W.3).
141 Milton, G. W., "The Care of the Dying," *Medical Journal of Australia*, 1972, vol. 2, p. 177.
142 Mitchell, W., "Local Government Services," *B.M.J.*, 1973, vol. 1, p. 39.
143 Moore, E. G., "Doctor's duty and patients' secrets" (Letter to *The Times*, 9th March, 1971).
144 Moore, E. G., Reported in Newsletter No. 20, April 1972, of the Institute of Religion and Medicine (see ref. 13).
145 Moore, W. R., "A First Glance at Terminal Care," *Journal of the Royal College of General Practitioners*, 1971, vol. 21, p. 387.
146 Moreton, V., "At St. Christopher's Hospice," *Physiotherapy*, June 1969.
147 Moritz, A. R., "Sudden Death," *New England Journal of Medicine*, 1940, vol. 223, no. 20, p. 798.
148 Morris, J. C., "The Management of Cases in the Terminal Stages of Malignant Disease," *St. Mary's Hospital Gazette*, 1959, vol. 65, p. 4.
149 Muras, H., "The Terminal Care of the Cancer Patient—The Almoner," *St. Mary's Hospital Gazette*, 1961, vol. 67, p. 121.

150 Nagy, M. H., "The Child's Theories Concerning Death," *Journal of Genetic Psychology*, 1948, vol. 73, p. 3.

151 Natterson, J. M. and Knudson, A. G., "Observations Concerning Fear of Death in Fatally Ill Children and Their Mothers," *Psychosomatic Medicine*, 1960, vol. 22, p. 456.

152 Naylor, V. M. and Michaels, D., *The Sufferings of the Cancer Patient*. (Published privately by Hutchinson Benham, 1967. There is a copy in the library at St. Bartholomew's Hospital, London.)

153 *New York Times*, American Euthanasia Society report (27th January, 1939).

154 Nightingale, F., *The Art of Nursing* (London, 1859), ch. 13.

155 Ogilvie, H., "Journey's End," *Practitioner*, 1957, vol. 179, p. 584.

156 Page, I. H., "Death and the Practitioner," *Modern Medicine*, July, 1970.

157 Parker-Rhodes, D., "The Mysticism of Death," *The Friend*, 23rd July, 1965 (from Friends' House, ref. 64).

158 Parkes, C. M., "Recent Bereavement as a Cause of Mental Illness," *British Journal of Psychiatry*, 1964, vol. 110, p. 198.

159 Parkes, C. M., "Bereavement and Mental Illness," *British Journal of Medical Psychology*, 1965, vol. 38, p. 1.

160 Parkes, C. M., "Broken Heart," *B.M.J.*, 1969, vol. 1, p. 740.

161 Parkes, C. M., "The First Year of Bereavement," *Psychiatry*, 1970, vol. 33, p. 444.

162 Parkes, C. M., *Feelings of Mutilation and Grief Following Loss of Limb, Spouse or Home* (Lecture to Society for Psychosomatic Research, London, 1st October, 1971).

163 Parkes, C. M., "Accuracy of Predictions of Survival in Later Stages of Cancer," *B.M.J.*, 1972, vol. 2, p. 29.

164 Parkes, C. M., *The Nature of Grief and the Reaction to Bereavement in Adult Life* (see ref. 13).

165 Paton, A., "Personal View," *B.M.J.*, 1969, vol. 3, p. 591.

166 Perkins, G., "Resuscitation," *Lancet*, 1967, vol. 2, p. 388.

167 Personal Paper, "Death of a Mind," *Lancet*, 1950, vol. 1, p. 1012.

168 Pickering, G., "Medicine and Society," *B.M.J.*, 1971, vol. 1, p. 191.

169 Pilcher, R. S., Address on his retirement from the Professorship of Surgery at University College Hospital, 20th October, 1967.

170 Pius XII, *Concerning Re-animation* (Address to the International Congress of Anaesthetists, translated in Catholic Truth Society booklet *The Relief of Pain*.)

171 Platt, R., "Reflections on Aging and Death," *Lancet*, 1963, vol. 1, p. 1.

172 Player, A., "Casework in Terminal Illness," *Almoner*, 1954, vol. 6, p. 477.

173 Pliny, Epistles I:22.

174 Porter, K. R. O., "Four Recurring Themes," *B.M.J.*, 1973, vol. 1, p. 40.

175 Rayport, M., "Addiction Problems in the Medical Use of Narcotic Analgesics," *Journal of Chronic Diseases*, 1956, vol. 4, p. 102.

176 Rees, W. D., "Personal View," *B.M.J.*, 1971, vol. 2, p. 164.
177 Rees, W. D., "The Hallucinations of Widowhood," *B.M.J.*, 1971, vol. 4, p. 37.
178 Rees, W. D., "The Distress of Dying," *B.M.J.*, 1972, vol. 3, p. 105.
179 Rees, W. D. and Lutkins, S. G., "Mortality of Bereavement," *B.M.J.*, 1967, vol. 4, p. 13.
180 Registrar General, *Statistical Review of England and Wales, 1962–67* (H.M.S.O.).
181 Riding, J. E., "The Outpatient Pain Clinic," *Journal of the Royal College of Surgeons of Ireland*, 1966, vol. 2, p. 279.
182 Robbie, D. S., *The Pain Clinic in a Cancer Hospital*, 1968 (Excerpta Medica International Congress Series No. 200, p. 961–3).
183 Robbie, D. S., *Management of Intractable Pain in Advanced Cancer of the Rectum* (Proceedings of Royal Society of Medicine: Supplement to vol. 63, p. 115).
184 Russell, W. R., *Discussion on the Treatment of Intractable Pain* (Proceedings of Royal Society of Medicine, 1959, vol. 52, pp. 983).
185 Russell, J. K. and Miller, M. R., "Care of Women with Terminal Pelvic Cancer," *B.M.J.*, 1964, vol. 1, p. 1214.
186 St. John-Stevas, N., "Dying in Peace" (Letter to *The Times*, 25th March, 1969).
187 St. Joseph's Hospice, *Christian Teaching Concerning Death* (see Ref. 17).
188 Saunders, C. M., *Treatment of Intractable Pain in Terminal Cancer* (Proceedings of Royal Society of Medicine, 1963, vol. 56, p. 191).
189 Saunders, C. M., *The Need for Institutional Care for the Patient with Advanced Cancer* (Cancer Institute, Madras, 1964. Copies from St. Christopher's Hospice. See Ref. 92.)
190 Saunders, C. M., "The Symptomatic Treatment of Incurable Malignant Disease," *Prescribers' Journal*, 1964, vol. 4, p. 68.
191 Saunders, C. M., "Telling Patients," *District Nursing*, 1965, vol. 8, p. 149.
192 Saunders, C. M., "The Last Stages of Life," *American Journal of Nursing*, March, 1965, vol. 65, no. 3.
193 Saunders, C. M., "A Medical Director's View" in *Death and Responsibility* (see ref. 105).
194 Saunders, C. M., "St. Christopher's Hospice," *British Hospital Journal and Social Service Review*, 10th November, 1967.
195 Saunders, C. M., "The Care of the Dying," *Gerontologia Clinica*, 1967, vol. 9, p. 6.
196 Saunders, C. M., *The Care of the Terminal Stages of Cancer* (Annals of Royal College of Surgeons, Supplement to vol. 41, 1967, p. 162).
197 Saunders, C. M., *The Management of Fatal Illness in Childhood* (Proceedings of Royal Society of Medicine, 1969, vol. 62, p. 550).
198 Saunders, C. M., In *Concord* (magazine of the English Speaking Union, 28th January, 1970).
199 Saunders, C. M., *The Patient's Response to Treatment* (Cancer Care Inc., symposium, October 1971).

200 Saunders, C. M. and Winner, A. L., "A Patient's Trust" (Letter to *The Times*, 23rd March, 1969).

201 Seal, P. V., "A Fatal Case of Carcinoma in a Young Man," *Journal of the College of General Practitioners*, 1965, vol. 10, p. 310.

202 Sholin, P. D., "Death of a Son," *Woman's Own*, 10th December, 1968.

203 Slater, E. T. O., *The Case for Voluntary Euthanasia* (Voluntary Euthanasia Society, see Ref. 56).

204 Slater, E. T. O., "Health Service or Sickness Service?" *B.M.J.*, 1971, vol. 4, p. 734.

205 Smith and Nephew, Postal Symposium of 1,150 General Practitioners, December, 1970.

206 Smithers, D. W., *A Clinical Prospect of the Cancer Problem* (Livingstone, 1960, p. 150).

207 Smithers, D. W., "Where to Die," *B.M.J.*, 1973, vol. 1, p. 34.

208 Spinks, M. E., "It *Has* Happened to Me," *Nursing Times*, 9th April, 1970.

209 Sprott, N. A., *Dying of Cancer* (The Medical Press, 1949, vol. 221, p. 187).

210 Suicide Act, 3rd August, 1961, clause 2.

211 *Sunday Times*, "Death and the Doctor's Duty" (20th August, 1972).

212 *Sunderland Echo*, Letter to Editor, 2nd August, 1972.

213 Sutton, M., "Enlightened Attitude to Cancer," *B.M.J.*, 1971, vol. 2, p. 336.

214 Sweetingham, C. R., "Questions of Confidence" (Letter to *The Times*, 25th March, 1969).

215 Tanner, E. R., "A Dedicated Nurse?" *Nursing Times*, 18th February, 1971.

216 Tanner, E. R., "Prolongation of Life," *Nursing Times*, 8th June, 1972.

217 Tanner, E. R., "The Postponement of Death in Old People," *Guy's Gazette*, 7th October, 1972.

218 Tanner, E. R., *A Time to Die* (St. Joseph's Hospice, occasional paper, 1973).

219 *The Times*, "The Taking of Life," 7th April, 1970.

220 *The Times*, Correspondence "Let These Children Die," August, 1972.

221 Townsend, P., *The Last Refuge* (Routledge & Kegan Paul, 1962).

222 Trowell, H. C., "Claiming the Right to Die" (Letter to *The Times*, 22nd April, 1970).

223 Trowell, H. C., Three Seminars on Prolonging Life in Unconscious Patients or in Elderly Persons (Institute of Religion and Medicine: see Ref. 13).

224 Twycross, R. G., "Euthanasia—An Alternative View," *Oxford Medical School Gazette*, 1964, vol. 16, p. 103.

225 Twycross, R. G., "Principles and Practice of the Relief of Pain in Terminal Cancer," *Update*, July, 1972.

226 Twycross, R. G., "How Steroids Can Help Terminal Cancer Patients," *General Practitioner*, 18th August, 1972.

227 Twycross, R. G., *Medical Critic of Working Party on Euthanasia* (Methodist Recorder, 7 June 1973).
228 Vere, D. W., *Should Christians Support Voluntary Euthanasia?* (Christian Medical Fellowship pamphlet from 56 Kingsway, London W.C.2).
229 Vere, D. W., Lecture to the Christian Medical Fellowship, 4th November, 1971.
230 Voluntary Euthanasia Bill, B.S. 96/1 1968–9:4.
231 Voluntary Euthanasia Society, *A Plea for Legislation to Permit Voluntary Euthanasia* (1970): from the Society, see Ref. 56.
232 Voluntary Euthanasia Society, *Doctors and Euthanasia* (1971).
233 Wallace, L., "The Needs of the Dying," *Nursing Times*, 13th November, 1969.
234 Weatherhead, L. D., "Claiming the Right to Die" (Letter to *The Times*, 17th April, 1970).
235 Weisman, A. D. and Hackett, T. P., "Predilection to Death," *Psychosomatic Medicine*, 1961, vol. 23, p. 232.
236 Welldon, R. M. C., "Living With Death" (Part 56, *Book of Life*, Marshall Cavendish encyclopaedia, 1969).
237 Welldon, R. M. C., "Bearing the Unbearable" (Part 97, *Book of Life*; see ref. 236).
238 Welldon, R. M. C., "The 'Shadow of Death' and its Implications in Four Families, Each with a Hospitalized Schizophrenic Member," *Family Process*, 1971, vol. 10, p. 281.
239 White, D., "Death Control," *New Society*, 30th November, 1972.
240 Whitehorn, K., "We All Run Away, but Can't Escape (*Observer*, 14th January, 1968).
241 Wilkes, E., Cancer Outside Hospital," *Lancet*, 1964, vol. 1, p. 1379.
242 Wilkes, E., "Terminal Cancer at Home," *Lancet*, 1965, vol. 1, p. 799.
243 Wilkes, E., "Where to Die," *B.M.J.*, 1973, vol. 1, p. 32.
244 Williams, G., *Euthanasia* (Royal Society of Medicine, 1970, vol. 63, p. 663).
245 Wilson, F. G., "Social Isolation and Bereavement," *Lancet*, 1970, vol. 2, p. 1356.
246 Winner, A. L., "Death and Dying," *Journal of the Royal College of Physicians of London*, 1970, vol. 4, no. 4, p. 351.
247 *Wolverhampton Express & Star*, "Answer to 'Let These Children Die' " (19th August, 1972).
248 Yale R., "The Terminal Care of the Cancer Patient—The Hospital Chaplain," *St. Mary's Hospital Gazette*, 1961, vol. 67, p. 123.
249 Yudkin, S., "Children and Death," *Lancet*, 1967, vol. 1, p. 37.
250 Zinsser, H., *Spring, Summer and Autumn* (*Poems*, Alfred A. Knopf, Inc., 1942, New York).

Bibliography

Autton, Norman, *The Pastoral Care of the Dying* (SPCK, London 1966). *The Pastoral Care of the Bereaved* (SPCK, 1967); and *From Fear to Faith* (SPCK, 1971).

Bayly, Joseph, *The Last Thing We Talk About—A Christian View of Death* (Scripture Union, 1970. From 5 Wigmore Street, London W.1).

Collin, Rodney, *The Theory of Eternal Life* (Stuart & Watkins, London, 1956).

Cope, Gilbert, *Dying, Death, and Disposal* (SPCK, London, 1970).

Church of England Information Office, booklet on *Decisions about life and death*, 1965).

Downing, A. B., *Euthanasia and the Right to Death* (Peter Owen, London, 1969).

Gavey, C. J., *The Management of the "Hopeless" Case* (H. K. Lewis, London, 1952).

Gibran, Kahlil, *The Prophet* (Heinemann, 1926).

Gould, Jonathan, *Your Death Warrant?* (Geoffrey Chapman, 1971).

Hinton, John, *Dying* (Penguin, 1967).

Conference report: *The Hour of our Death* (Geoffrey Chapman, 1973).

Hyams, Dennis, *The Care of the Aged* (Priory, 1973).

Kelly, Kevin T., *Euthanasia* (Catholic Truth Society No. S285. From 201 Victoria Street, London, S.W.1).

Kübler-Ross, Elisabeth, *On Death and Dying* (Tavistock Publications, London, 1970).

Lewis, C. S., *The Problem of Pain* (Fontana, 1940).

Lewis, C. S., *A Grief Observed* (Faber & Faber, 1961).

Martin, Eva, *The Ring of Return* (Philip Allen, 1927).

Mitford, J., *The American Way of Death* (Hutchinson, 1963).

Parkes, Colin Murray, *Bereavement* (Tavistock Publications, 1972).

Pearson, L., *Death and Dying* (Case Western Reserve University, Cleveland, Ohio, 1969).

British Medical Association report, 1971: *The Problems of Euthanasia*.

Booklet, *The Problem of Euthanasia* (London Medical Group and the Society for the Study of Medical Ethics, 1972).

St. John-Stevas, Norman, *The Right to Life* (Hodder, 1963).

Saunders, Cicely M., *The Management of Terminal Illness* (Hospital Medicine, 1967).

Saunders, Cicely M., "Care of the Dying," *Nursing Times* reprint.

Shotter, Edward F., *Matters of Life and Death* (Darton, Longman & Todd, London, 1970).

Snell, Beatrice Saxon, *Horizon*, an anthology (Friends' Home Service, Friends' House, Euston Road, London N.W.1).

Stephens, Simon, *Death Comes Home* (Mowbrays, 1972).

Torrie, Margaret, *Begin Again—a book for Women alone* (Dent, 1970).

Trowell, Hugh, *The Unfinished Debate on Euthanasia* (S.C.M. Press, 58 Bloomsbury Street, London W.C.1, 1973).

Vere, Duncan W., *Voluntary Euthanasia—is there an Alternative?* (Christian Medical Fellowship Press, 56 Kingsway, London W.C.2, 1971).

Williams, Glanville, *The Sanctity of Life and the Criminal Law* (Faber & Faber, 1958).

Worcester, Alfred, *The Care of the Aged, the Dying and the Dead* (Blackwell Scientific Publications, Oxford, 1935).

Index